"Fortunately, I am prepared to do the decent thing."

Bethany swung around to look at him in surprise. "Do the decent thing? What are you talking about?"

"You are pregnant with my baby and I am a man of honor—a man who takes his responsibilities seriously. Naturally, I have no other option but to marry you."

"*Marry me?* Have you completely lost your mind?" Bethany gave a snort of laughter. Did he really expect her to leap at his generous offer because he was *a man of honor,* who *took his responsibilities seriously* and would therefore rise to the occasion by putting a ring on her finger because there was no option?

"What are you saying?" With one hand, Cristiano reached to the side of the bed and flipped on the light. Immediately the tiny area around them was thrown into relief. He hoisted himself on one elbow and looked down at her with a cold frown of incomprehension.

"I'm saying that I'm not going to marry you!"

All about the author...
Cathy Williams

CATHY WILLIAMS was born in the West Indies and has been writing Harlequin romances for some fifteen years. She is a great believer in the power of perseverance, as she had never written anything before (apart from school essays a lifetime ago!), and from the starting point of zero has now fulfilled her ambition to pursue this most enjoyable of careers. She would encourage any would-be writer to have faith and go for it!

She lives in the beautiful Warwickshire countryside with her husband and three children, Charlotte Olivia and Emma. When not writing she is hard-pressed to find a moment's free time in between the millions of household chores, not to mention being a one-woman taxi service for her daughters' never-ending social lives.

She derives inspiration from the hot, lazy, tropical island of Trinidad (where she was born), from the peaceful countryside of middle England and, of course, from her many friends, who are a rich source of plots and are particularly garrulous when it comes to describing Harlequin Presents heroes. It would seem from their complaints that tall, dark and charismatic men are way too few and far between! Her hope is to continue writing romance fiction and providing those eternal tales of love for which, she feels, we all strive.

Cathy Williams

ONE NIGHT IN ROME

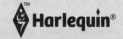

Harlequin®

TORONTO NEW YORK LONDON
AMSTERDAM PARIS SYDNEY HAMBURG
STOCKHOLM ATHENS TOKYO MILAN MADRID
PRAGUE WARSAW BUDAPEST AUCKLAND

Recycling programs
for this product may
not exist in your area.

ISBN-13: 978-0-373-13036-8

ONE NIGHT IN ROME
Previously published in the U.K. as *The Italian's One-Night Love-Child*

First North American Publication 2011

Copyright © 2009 by Cathy Williams

ONE NIGHT IN ROME

CHAPTER ONE

COCOONED in the pleasantly cold confines of his black Mercedes, Cristiano De Angelis surveyed the hustle and bustle of the scorchingly hot streets around him from behind a pair of dark designer sunglasses. This part of Rome was as familiar to him as his own penthouse apartment in London where he lived for most of the year, occasionally taking time out to visit his family in Italy. He had grown up here, had gone to school here, had enjoyed the gilded life of a member of the Italian elite, only spreading his wings when he had flown off to go to university in England. It was both comforting and a little claustrophobic to be back, even for a week, and it would be something of a relief to return to the relative anonymity granted him in the streets of London.

He frowned, thinking back to the conversation he had just had with his mother and his grandfather, who had conspired to remind him, over a sumptuous lunch served with unnecessary formality in the opulent dining room of his grandfather's house, of the passage of time, in so far as it affected him and the pitter patter of small De Angelis feet which they were both, it seemed, desperate to hear.

It had been a dual assault of military precision with his mother on the one side, virtually wringing her hands as she elaborated on her maternal desire that he settle down, be happy, stop playing the field, while his grandfather chipped in with guilt-inducing asides about his declining health and old age, as though he was a decrepit centenarian and not the sprightly seventy-eight-year-old man who could still command attention without uttering a word.

'There's a very nice girl…' his mother had begun, assessing whether that casual piece of information might have landed on fertile ground, but Cristiano had not been having it. While he acknowledged that he would, indeed, one day get married to someone suitable, that time had not quite arrived. He had been firm on the point and, of course, it had been regrettable that he had been forced to witness their crestfallen faces, but the pair of them, given half a chance, would have proved more unstoppable than a freight train at full speed. Any hint of softening on his part and they would have been lining up prospective candidates within minutes.

A reluctant smile of wry amusement curved his mouth and he removed his shades, dangling them from one finger as he looked at the hordes of shoppers who swarmed the elegant designer shop-lined streets, for all the world as though the words *credit crunch* were not part of their vocabulary.

Without giving himself time to change his mind, he tapped on the glass partition separating him from his driver and leaned forward to tell Enrico that he could let him out here.

'Take the car back to my place,' Cristiano said, grimacing at the prospect of having to brave the sweltering summer sun but recognising that if he didn't do it then he would be stuck in traffic for the foreseeable future and, comfortable though it was inside the Mercedes, he couldn't afford to waste time sitting in it for the next hour or so. 'I have to deliver this for my mother and it will be quicker for me to take to the back streets than for you to drive me there. I'll get a taxi back.'

'But sir, the sun…'

Enrico, who had been the family driver for as long as Cristiano could remember, looked faint at the thought of his passenger stepping out into the sweltering heat, and Cristiano grinned.

'I'm not a swooning Victorian maiden, Enrico,' he said drily. 'I think I'll be able to withstand half an hour out there. After all, look at the shoppers. No one seems to be collapsing from heat exhaustion.'

'But sir, those are women. They are built to shop in all weather without being affected…'

Cristiano was still grinning as he strode out into the blistering sun, sunglasses firmly back in place. He was aware, and chose to ignore, the sidelong glances of women as he walked past. He was pretty sure that if he slowed his pace it wouldn't be long before some long-legged, dark-haired, pedigreed beauty approached him. Even though he no longer resided in the city, his face was well known in certain circles. Visits to Rome were seldom free from glittering invitations from women who courted his company, usually without success because, despite his mother's accusations, he was discerning in his choices. Which, as he began leaving the crowded shopping quarter, brought him right back to thinking about her matchmaking designs. He had had no scarring emotional involvements with any woman. He had nothing against the institution of marriage, per se. Nor did he envisage a life without children, despite the manner in which he had earlier brushed aside the subject with an indolent wave of his hand. Cristiano could only think that he had been thoroughly ruined by his parents' happy marriage. Was that possible? Wasn't it supposed to work the other way around? They had been childhood sweethearts, perfectly matched in every way and, as if plucked from a fairy story, had lived perfectly happy lives until his father had died five years previously. His mother still wore black, carried pictures of him in her handbag and frequently referred to him in the present tense.

In an age of quickie divorces, money-grabbing gold-diggers and women with an eye to the main chance, what hope in hell did he have of a comparable marriage?

It took him a little over twenty minutes before he was standing in front of the gracious block of apartments where he had been instructed to hand deliver a very delicate orchid to one of the women who had helped out two weeks previously on a charity fund-raiser, a belated thank you present for her contribution. His mother was leaving for their country house and the orchid, she told him, *would not wait* until she returned. Nor would she trust any old courier service to deliver it because those *ragamuffin boys* were useless when it came to delivering anything *of a fragile nature*.

Privately, Cristiano figured that it was her way of expressing her pique at his casual dismissal of whatever suitable candidate she had had lined up her sleeve for his perusal, but running the errand had been a small price to pay for making good his escape.

Nor had the walk been half as uncomfortable as he had imagined. He very rarely *walked* anywhere, he realised. His life was cushioned by the luxury of a full-time driver in London and, besides, walking for the sake of walking was a time-consuming business in a life that seemed to have little spare time as it was.

The block of opulent apartments was portered and he was pointed in the direction of the lift without question. Even dressed in casual clothes, Cristiano exuded the sort of wealth, power and confidence that ensured entry anywhere.

The porter had asked for no identification and Cristiano would have been outraged had his movements been questioned.

Rather than take the lift, though, he decided to climb the three flights up to the apartment. This was no dingy staircase. Rich turquoise carpeting ran its length and the wallpaper was cool and sophisticated. He assumed the apartment would be more of the same. In all events, several rings on the doorbell elicited no response. Nor did his mother's mobile when he called to inform her that his mission had been a waste of time.

What the hell was he to do, stranded with an overpriced hothouse plant in search of a home?

Cursing under his breath for having allowed himself to be virtually blackmailed into running the ridiculous errand, he finally resorted to banging on the door. Like every single mega-expensive apartment building on the face of the earth, there was an eerie silence in the hall. He knew from his own personal experience that rich people rarely emerged to chew the fat and pass the time of day with the people living in the apartments next to them. He, frankly, had no time for useless chatter on stairwells or in elevators and happily was spared such inconvenience by having a private lift to his penthouse apartment.

He banged on the door again, this time very loudly, and was rewarded with the sound of scurrying feet.

Under normal circumstances, Bethany, hearing those three *ridiculously loud and incredibly rude* bangs would have flown to the door, prepared to give her unwanted caller a piece of her mind, but as it was these weren't exactly normal circumstances.

In fact…

She glanced down at what she was wearing and broke out in a fine film of nervous perspiration. The dress, which must have set its owner back the price of a small car, clung lovingly to her body, graceful, floaty and as utterly, utterly beautiful on as it had been hanging in the wardrobe fifteen minutes earlier.

Oh, God, why, why, *why* had she given in to the temptation to just *try it on*? What had possessed her? She had managed to resist the urge for the past three days, so why now? Because, she thought frantically, it had been so hot outside and she had come back to the apartment and had a long, luxurious bubbly bath in the splendid marbled bathroom and then she had strolled into the dressing room, which was three times the size of the poky room she had been renting at university, and she had run her hands along the magnificent gowns and dresses and jackets and coats and had stopped at this particular creation and had just not been able to resist the wicked impulse.

Now, having ignored the doorbell, there was some persistent visitor banging like mad on the door and she knew for a fact that it wouldn't be Amy, who had gone to Florence for the weekend with her boyfriend. Nor would it be a salesman because they weren't allowed to set foot into the hallowed halls of the building. Which just left…*a resident* or, worse yet, *a friend*.

The fourth bang snapped her out of her merciless day-dream, which involved first and foremost losing her job as house-sitter, which was a laugh considering Amy should have been the one doing it, followed rapidly by angry Italian policemen and a stint in a cell somewhere.

She stood behind the door and opened it very, very slowly, making sure that none of her body in its borrowed garb was revealed. Her eyes travelled from the ground upwards. And upwards. From expensive tan loafers and cream trousers towards a similarly cream collared polo shirt, taking in the tanned arms, the dark hair curling round

the dull silver of a very expensive make of watch, up to...
the most amazing face she had ever set eyes on in her entire
life. In fact, the stranger standing outside the front door
was so sensationally handsome that, for a few seconds,
Bethany felt literally winded.

Then reality kicked in and she remembered where she
was. In an apartment that wasn't hers and decked out in
clothes that weren't hers. She edged further behind the
safety of the heavy door.

'Yes? May I help you?' She didn't want to stare, but she
found that it was practically impossible not to. It wasn't just
the man's height, and he must be over six foot, nor was it
the perfection of his features or the sculpted muscularity
of his body. It was the aura of power and incredible self-
assurance that invested him with a potent, suffocating sex
appeal.

Cristiano, initially taken aback by the woman who had
answered the door, a girl when he had been expecting an
ageing dowager, was now busy taking in the delicate lines
of her heart-shaped face, the full mouth, the slanting green
eyes and the mass of copper hair that tumbled down, almost
to her waist.

'Are you *hiding*?' he asked and was fascinated as a tide
of pale pink coloured her cheeks. Nor was she responding
as women usually did at his presence, with smiles and
lowered lashes and all those coy signals that indicated
interest.

'Hiding?' His voice matched his looks. Deep, lazy, confident. 'I'm not hiding.' Bethany sidled a little further along
so that the wretched dress was not at all visible. She didn't
know who this man was but if he lived here, if he was a
friend, he would know that she certainly wasn't the Amelia
Doni who owned the apartment and who was in her mid
forties. He might, however, know that the outrageously

expensive dress would not belong to a twenty-one-year-old girl who happened to be house-sitting. 'I'm just a little surprised…to have a visitor…I'm sorry, I don't know your name…'

'Cristiano De Angelis.' He waited for a glimmer of recognition because any woman who owned this apartment would have heard of the De Angelis family. He wondered how it was that he had not met her before at one of the high society events that he invariably attended when he came to Rome to spend time with his family. This was a face he certainly would have remembered. She was not the usual Italian beauty, although her Italian was fluent. She looked… It suddenly dawned on him why he might not have met her in the past and he smiled slowly, switching effortlessly from Italian to English.

'And now that I have introduced myself, perhaps you'd like to tell me if I'm at the right apartment…Signora Doni?'

'I'm sorry. You haven't told me what you're doing here.'

Cristiano produced the orchid, the existence of which he had temporarily forgotten. 'From my mother.'

Bethany stared blankly at him and, as the cogs in her brain began whirring back into life, she realised that he didn't know who she was. He was a man on an errand and had no idea what Amelia Doni looked like. Ergo, he would not be rounding on her for having sneakily taken advantage of her second-hand house-sitting to don some fancy clothing. She relaxed slightly and stuck her hand out for the plant.

'Great. Thanks.'

Great? Thanks? Shouldn't she be inviting him in? At least showing some semblance of interest in getting to know who he was?

'It's a little ridiculous to be having a conversation like this,' Cristiano drawled. 'Why don't you invite me in? After all, I've just spent the past twenty-five minutes in baking sun to walk over here and deliver a potted plant. I could really do with something cold to drink.' He was a little incredulous that she actually spent a few seconds mentally debating whether or not she should open the door and let him in.

'You may not have heard of me, but let me assure you that the De Angelis are a well known family in Italy. There's no need to fear for your life or your possessions.' Since when did he give long spiels about his background to anyone? In fact, when was the last time he had ever found himself in the company of a woman who looked at him as though he might leap out and attack her at any moment? In a word, never.

'I don't.' She breathed a little easier. 'I've been brought up never to talk to strangers.'

'I introduced myself. I'm therefore no longer a stranger. You also know my mother, if only casually…' He smiled and Bethany's entire nervous system seemed to go into immediate meltdown. Her skin tingled, her throat went dry and her breasts felt suddenly hypersensitive, her nipples hardening and aching at the same time.

This was not a familiar response for Bethany. In fact, she had always been comfortable around the opposite sex. She could chat with them, tease them, even assess them without this sensation of drowning. Sandwiched between her intellectually gifted older sister and a younger sister whose radiant beauty had had boys banging on the front door from the age of eleven, Bethany had happily occupied the middle ground, content with being reasonably clever and averagely, in her eyes, attractive. From her comfortable background position, she had been able to watch Shania,

wrapped up in her elitist world of books and heavily intel-
lectual boyfriends, and Melanie, prancing from one dishy
guy to another and changing them with the sort of regularity that other women changed outfits. She had learnt to
chat to both sets of boyfriends without treading on either
of her sisters' toes. She was therefore a little shocked and
taken aback by the way this tall, dark, lean and stagger-
ingly good-looking stranger was managing to throw her
into turmoil.

'Okay. I guess you can come in for a moment,' she conceded nervously. 'It's really hot out there. I can get you a
glass of water, if you like…' She pulled open the door and
stood aside to let him sweep past her. Looking down, she
spied the dainty strappy sandals on her feet. It now seemed
highly unfortunate that the absentee owner of the apartment
was roughly her size.

'Nice place.' Cristiano gave the apartment a cursory
once-over. He had been brought up in palatial surroundings. Other people's displays of wealth had always failed
to impress him. 'How long have you lived here?' He had
swivelled back round to look at her and her impact on him
was such that for a millisecond time seemed to stand still.
Her eyes had to be the clearest green he had ever seen and
her tumble of copper hair was a stunning contrast to the
creamy paleness of her skin. The sprinkling of freckles,
paradoxically, added a freshness to her beauty, rescued her
from being just another attractive face. And he had no idea
why she had been so keen to hide away behind the door
when she had first opened it. Her body was magnificent.
Slender but full breasted and, judging from the dress, this
was a lady who had taste.

'How long have I lived here?' Bethany repeated, parrot
fashion. 'Not long.' Literally. 'I'll get you some water. If
you just want to…um…stay right here. Won't be long…'

'You look as though you're dressed to go out. Have I caught you at a bad time?' He looked at her with gleaming eyes, sidelining his curiosity at her bizarre behaviour in favour of playing with the thought that he might be tempted to turn this casual meeting into something a little more rewarding. It wasn't often that he was put in the position of pursuit. It was even less often that his initial response to a woman was so immediate. He found that he was enjoying both experiences.

'Dressed to go out?' Bethany made a big effort and dragged her eyes away from him so that she could teeter in her borrowed heels towards the kitchen.

'Are you always this jumpy?'

Bethany, in the process of getting some bottled water from the fridge, invested his passing remark with bullseye accuracy as she, on cue, jumped, because she hadn't been aware of him following her into the kitchen.

'Would you mind not creeping around like that?' she said tersely. 'Here. Water.' She shoved the glass out to him and, once relieved of it, folded her arms.

'Do you have a first name, Miss Doni?' Getting anything out of this woman was like pulling teeth. His own white ones gritted together with irritation.

'Why would you want to know my name?' A trail of possible consequences crawled into her mind with poisonous clarity. The house-sitting job had originally fallen to one of the owner's relatives, who happened to be a friend of Amy's. Bethany wasn't too sure why the girl had handed over the responsibility to Amy, but Amy had then delegated it to Bethany because she had landed herself a boyfriend and wasn't happy about committing a month of her summer holiday to being cooped up in Rome. Bethany had been overjoyed at the arrangement. She would get to practise her Italian in the most beautiful city in the world and, furthermore, would have free accommodation in the sort of place she would never have clapped eyes on, never mind *lived in*, in a million years. *And* she would be paid for her trouble! Revealing her identity would be step one to landing her in a great deal of difficulty and, worse than that, would land Amy and her friend in even more trouble. She felt faint and half closed her eyes and leaned heavily against the kitchen counter.

'Are you all right?'

Bethany opened her eyes to find him standing disconcertingly close to her, which made her feel flustered and breathless, but she kept her voice even when she replied. 'Fine. I'm fine.' She shifted a bit and Cristiano frowned, irritated by that small gesture of flight.

'You don't look fine. Your colour's up. Maybe it's the heat out there. You're very fair. Italian women are accustomed to the heat in Rome over the summer months, but then you're not Italian, are you? Despite the fact that you speak the language fluently. Is this…' he looked around at the superbly kitted kitchen, which bore all the hallmarks of somewhere that was underused '…a holiday place?'

Bethany could only stare. Did people have *holiday places* that looked like this? Marble everywhere? Paintings on the walls that cost the earth? A dressing room stuffed to overflowing with fabulous designer clothes?

He settled that score by adding, 'I myself have several.'

'Do you?' She sidestepped the question and was relieved when he broke the hold he had on her with his eyes by tipping his head back to swallow some water.

Cristiano shrugged. 'Here. Paris. New York. Barbados. Of course, Paris and New York are largely used when I'm over there on business. It's useful not having to book hotels whenever I'm abroad.' He dumped the glass on the counter, determined to bring the conversation back to *her*. 'So your name…'

'Amelia,' Bethany told him miserably, crossing her fingers behind her back.

'And where do you permanently reside, Amelia Doni?'

'London.'

'You're not a very forthcoming person, are you, Miss Amelia Doni? I take it you *are* a miss…? I don't notice a wedding ring on your hand.'

'If you're finished with that water…'

Far from sounding flattered at his interest, she seemed even more keen to shepherd him out of the apartment, and it set his teeth on edge with rampant irritation.

'How long are you over here?' Cristiano asked because, perversely, the more disinterested she seemed, the more determined he became to break through her invisible silent barrier.

Bethany shrugged and muttered something along the lines of *not very long*.

'But presumably you were here long enough to get involved in the charity fund-raiser?'

'Charity fund-raiser?'

'The orchid? The one currently languishing on a table in the hall? It's a thank you present from my mother. You must know how much she contributes to charity and I gather the last fund-raiser was particularly successful. She would have delivered it to you herself but she's leaving for the country this evening and won't be back for a while.'

'Leaving for the country…' Bethany repeated, aware that she was beginning to sound like someone mentally challenged.

'We have a country house,' Cristiano elaborated, bemused by her complete lack of interest in anything he had to say. 'It's far cooler in the hills than it is in the city…'

'Yes, yes, I expect it would be. You must thank her for the…um…plant…'

'What was your role in the fund-raiser?'

'Ah…well…actually, I prefer not to hark back to things that have happened in the past. I'm a *live for today* kind of person…'

'My kind of woman. I'm not scheduled to return to London until tomorrow. Have dinner with me tonight.'

'What? No! No, no, no…!' Bethany was alternately appalled at the thought of being caught out and stunned by the realisation that *she wanted to accept his invitation*. She didn't know whether it was because she was in Italy and removed from her familiar comfort zone, but everything she was feeling and doing was horrendously out of character. 'You have to go,' she said in an agony of urgency.

'Why? Are you expecting someone? A man? Are you involved with anyone?'

'No.' She began walking towards the front door. Lying did not come naturally to her and she knew that it would be just a matter of time before she tripped herself up.

'So let's get this straight. You're not involved with anyone. You're not waiting for anyone. Why the reluctance to have dinner with me?'

'I…I…um…I think it's a bit rude for you to come here on an errand and then ask me out to dinner…'

'You mean you're not flattered?'

'I mean I don't know you…'

'So dinner would be the perfect opportunity to rectify that situation!' He noticed that he had somehow been manoeuvred towards the front door and her small, pale hand was very firmly round the door handle. He watched in disbelief as she began turning the knob. He had, literally, been shown the door!

'I don't think so, but thanks for the invitation anyway.

And…for the plant as well. I'll make sure that I look after it, although I've never been very good with plants.'

'Funny. Nor have I.' He leaned indolently against the door, making it impossible for her to open it. 'Already we have one thing in common.'

'Do you do this a lot?' Bethany asked, heart beating like a hammer inside her because something about him was sending her nervous system into overdrive. 'Pop in to random strangers' houses and ask them out to dinner? Okay, so it's not *rude* as such, but you have to admit that it's a bit *strange*. I mean…' she tested the water '…you don't know me from Adam. Goodness, I could be *anyone*!'

'Yes,' Cristiano said thoughtfully, 'you could be anyone. Axe-murderer, psychopath…' He shot her a curling smile that made her catch her breath. 'Worse than that, scheming gold-digger after my money…However, you do have certain credentials, namely your connection with my mother and…' he looked briefly around him, then back to her '…the fact that you own a place like this. Axe-murderers, psychopaths and gold-diggers probably wouldn't be into charity fund-raising or have holiday apartments in one of the best postcodes in Rome. So my fears are put to rest.'

Bethany was beginning to feel giddy from the torrent of misconceptions swimming around her. *Credentials? Knowing his mother? Owning the apartment?*

'And, admit it, you have to eat.'

'I…I actually don't like eating out. I prefer eating in. Cooking. So many wonderful fresh ingredients over here. It's fun to experiment.'

'Fine. I'll come here.'

'But you can't.' She stared up at the dangerously good-looking face gazing right back down at her and was overcome with the unusual sensation of walking on the very edge of a precipice. The view was tremendous, but falling was a real possibility.

'Of course I can.' Cristiano shrugged. Blessed with a lethal combination of looks, brains and wealth, he had yet to come across a member of the opposite sex who could resist him, and he refused to credit that the woman standing in front of him would prove to be the exception. 'I can either come here or I can pick you up at eight.'

'Why? Why do you want to take me out to dinner? Did your mother ask you to?'

'Why should she do that?' Cristiano's brows knitted into a perplexed frown. 'My mother has no involvement in my personal life and, in fact, she'll be very firmly ensconced in the country by the time I come over here later.' He pushed himself away from the door, not taking his eyes off her face. She really had the most marvellous skin. Translucent. Even without make-up. Not at all like the sultry brunettes he normally favoured. His mother had said very little about her but, then again, why should she have? It would seem that the woman was merely a friend of a friend of a friend who had been sequestered to help out for the charity bash, hence the orchid, which was an expensive but fairly impersonal way of demonstrating appreciation. Anyway, it was a good thing that nothing had been said because it would have been a sure-fire way of turning him off.

'All mothers have involvement in their children's lives,' Bethany was distracted enough to point out, thinking of her own mother who clucked and fussed and still sent food parcels in the post from Ireland just to make sure that she wasn't on the brink of starvation.

'When it comes to women, I keep things strictly to myself.' He opened the door, not allowing her the chance to become embroiled in a debate on a non-subject which would give her the opportunity to remember that she was busily trying to turn him down. He'd never been turned down. Furthermore, he had highly sensitised antennae and they were picking up her interest in him. He couldn't understand why she would try and fight something as innocent as a dinner date but, whatever her reasons, that wide-eyed way she kept backing away intrigued him. Of course, she could just be playing hard to get, but he seriously doubted that. She had a face that spoke volumes. In fact, he hadn't seen such an openly expressive face since…frankly, he couldn't remember. 'I should warn you that I usually get what I want,' he inserted without vanity.

'And you want dinner with me. Before you leave tomorrow.'

'Finally!' He gave her another of those amazing, toe-curling smiles. 'We have lift-off.' He took her hand, catching her by surprise, and turned it palm up so that he could press a brief kiss against her soft skin in a gesture that seemed purely, wickedly Italian and thrilled her to the bone.

'I suppose so. But…but it'll have to be an early night…' she said anxiously.

'You mean back home before the stroke of midnight when you revert to being a pumpkin?'

Bethany went bright red. She honestly couldn't say what had propelled her to accept the dinner invitation, but there was a trail of treacherous excitement curling inside her, starting at the tips of her toes, going right through her body to her dazed green eyes, which were locked onto his face with nervous fascination. Not even his quip about the pumpkin and midnight could wrench her from her foolhardy fascination and she was still feeling shell-shocked after he had gone.

It was only when she caught sight of herself in the floor to ceiling mirror in the bedroom that reality assaulted her with merciless clarity and she dialled Amy on her mobile phone.

She had to contain an impatient moan of pure frustration as Amy's excitable voice greeted her on the other end of the line with an enthusiastic rundown of her latest conquest and the fabulous Florentine sights, which they had yet to see because the bed was proving too alluring.

Bethany waited until she had run out of steam and then said hesitantly, 'Little problem on this end.' The floaty dress was still in evidence, witness to her moment of madness.

'Oh, God! Tell me the apartment hasn't burnt down!'

'Still in one piece. But there's been a visitor…and here's the thing…' The dress, which had seemed so temptingly beautiful, now stared balefully back at her from the mirror as she proceeded to tell her friend what had recently transpired. She kept getting muddled up because, in her head, all she could see was the stranger's lean, dark, outrageously sexy face looking at her in a way that was both intrusive and scarily exciting and nothing at all like the way other boys back home had ever looked at her.

'So you're going out with him for dinner… Oh, God, let me think…okay, okay…might be for the best…'

'Because…?'

Half an hour later, Bethany removed the offending dress, laid it on the bed because it would have to be dry-cleaned in the morning, and thought that there was a lot of truth about webs and lies and getting entangled. Catrina, the original house-sitter and cherished godchild of the hapless Amelia Doni, who was on a cruise a thousand miles away from Rome, was in London. In rehab. Very hush-hush, and all hell would break loose should loaded and doting godmother find out. So the task of house-sitting had fallen to Amy, with a code red level of secrecy but, Amy being Amy, Love had reared its head and her house-sitting mission had fallen quickly by the wayside. Thankfully, Bethany had been there, ever reliable and immune to being led astray. The sort of girl who enjoyed reading Italian books at night and thought that three glasses of wine qualified as a binge-drinking fest.

Now, as she stared down at the dress on the bed, Bethany wondered what had happened to Little Miss Reliability. The most daring thing she had done in ages had been to try that wretched dress on because yes, she really *did* enjoy curling up with a good book most nights and sometimes she even fulfilled that dreariest of clichés by curling up with a good book *and* a mug of hot chocolate.

But now she had accepted a dinner invitation from a guy who was sinfully sexy *and* ultra-sophisticated. Moreover, it was just going to be a one-night affair, and if, *for once*, she acted out of character, if she behaved like the kind of person who might conceivably have a holiday apartment dripping with designer clothes, the kind of woman who thought nothing of hanging around in a dress that cost a small fortune, then why not? She would be helping Amy out because no one, but *no one,* could get a *whiff* of Catrina drying out in a clinic in the UK and the *last thing* anyone needed was for some connected Italian guy to start asking questions.

Bethany felt a kick of excitement stir inside her. Of course, whatever she wore that night she would have dry-cleaned. She wasn't *that irresponsible*. She was just going to have a couple of hours of fun…no harm there…

CHAPTER TWO

'So...TELL me about yourself...'

It was an inevitable question but it still made Bethany's nerves jangle because after the initial crazy euphoria of wondering what it would be like to step into someone else's shoes for a night had come the shattering reality that she was, in actual fact, going to spend a few hours in the company of a sex god under false pretences. Between Cristiano's departure from the apartment and the sound of his voice four hours later on the intercom when he arrived to collect her, she had had ample time to concede that a man like him—sleek, sophisticated, extraordinarily handsome—would never have looked at a girl like her under normal circumstances. In fact, they would never even have *met* under normal circumstances.

Bethany, who had managed to fall back on most of her own clothes because leaving the house in someone else's wardrobe seemed a bit rich, all things considered, wondered how best to answer his question.

She finally settled on a vague, nonsensical answer along the lines of being a *free spirit*.

'What does that mean?' Cristiano looked across at her. She intrigued him and he had found himself looking forward to their dinner more than he had looked forward to any date with a woman in a long time. Nor had she disappointed. When the elevator doors had pinged open and she had walked across the marbled foyer towards him, he had literally been stopped in his tracks. She might have had all the money she wanted at her disposal, but she had foregone the diamonds and pearls, the little black dress that screamed *designer* and the killer stilettos, and instead had dressed down in a pair of jeans and some flat tan loafers with a pale blue wrap over her shoulders. Cristiano liked it. It took a confident woman to go for comfort and it took a sexy one to pull it off.

'What does that *mean*?' Bethany's natural warmth came out in her smile. Now that she was talking and not just gawping like a star-struck teenager, she could begin to relax a little and to enjoy the stolen moment in time. 'You sound like someone who's spent a lifetime living in a bubble.'

'Living in a bubble…' Cristiano looked at her thoughtfully. 'I suppose I *did* grow up in a bubble of sorts. Coming from a privileged background can have that effect. You're naturally supposed to do certain things…'

Bethany could only imagine. 'Like what?'

'Don't tell me you haven't experienced the same sort of thing. A certain lifestyle to which you conform, more or less, from an early age.'

Bethany thought of her own riotous Irish upbringing, the house always full of friends and family, boyfriends in and out, their two dogs and three cats and the general happy chaos that had made up her formative years. Conforming to anything from an early age was an alien concept.

'I'm more of a non-conformist,' she said truthfully. 'I mean, I'm not a wild child or anything like that, but I was never told that I had to be a certain way or do certain things.'

'Perhaps things work a little differently in your part of the world,' Cristiano murmured. 'Here, in Italy, I have always known what my future held in store for me.' They had drifted outside into a balmy summer evening.

'That must have been tough.'

'Tough? Why?' He was fascinated by the thought of any woman who could apply the adjective *tough* to any aspect of his life. Even the richest of women he had dated in the past had been impressed to death by the breadth of his power and privilege. 'Since when is it tough to have the world at your disposal?'

'No one has the world at their disposal!' Bethany laughed, as they began walking slowly towards his car, which he had parked, he had explained, in the only free space at the very end of the long road.

'You'd be surprised.'

Underneath the lazy, sexy timbre of his voice, she could detect the ruthless patina of a man accustomed to getting exactly what he wanted and she shivered. 'You just think you have the world at your disposal because everyone around you is primed to agree with everything you say,' she felt compelled to point out. 'I think it must be one of the downfalls of having too much money...'

'*Too much money?* I don't believe I've ever heard that expression cross a woman's lips.' He was privately amused that someone of presumably substantial private means could wax lyrical about *the pitfalls of wealth* but it was refreshing, for once, to find himself in the company of a woman who seemed to have a social conscience.

Bethany decided that if he was a learning curve for her, then why shouldn't she be a learning curve for him? What did she have to lose? She guessed instinctively that he wasn't a man who had much experience when it came to having his opinions questioned. The way he had asked her out to dinner, refused to concede that she might turn him down, indicated someone whose belief in the *whole world being at his disposal* was absolute.

'What type of women do you mix with?' Bethany asked, fascinated beyond belief by the wildly exotic creature looking lazily at her. His eyes were as dark as molasses, fringed by the most ridiculously long lashes imaginable, and the way his dark hair curled against the collar of his shirt, a little too long to be entirely conventional but not so long that he looked unkempt, brought her out in goosebumps.

Cristiano laughed and reached out to curl one finger into a strand of her copper hair. 'Always brunettes,' he murmured, 'although I'm beginning to wonder why. Is this the real colour of your hair?'

'Of course it is!' Excitement leapt inside her at his casual touch and her green eyes widened. 'Not *everyone* gets their hair colour from a bottle!'

'But quite a few do.' Her hair felt like silk between his fingers.

'So, in other words, you only go out with brunettes who dye their hair?'

'They tend to have other characteristics aside from the dyed hair.' He had an insane desire to yank her towards him and do what came naturally. Very unlike him. He reluctantly released the strands of hair and stood back just in case primitive instinct got the better of him. 'Long legs. Exquisite faces. Right background.'

'Right background?'

Cristiano shrugged. 'It's important,' he admitted. 'Life can be stressful enough without the added hassle of wondering whether the woman sharing your bed is more interested in your bank balance than in your company.'

Bethany's stomach gave a nervous flutter but she was reassured by the fact that she knew she definitely wasn't after his money. 'Maybe you're a little insecure.'

'*A little insecure?*' Cristiano looked at her with rampant incredulity. 'No. Insecurity has never been a problem for me,' he told her with satisfaction. 'And please tell me that you aren't going to spend the evening trying to analyse me.'

'Where are we going to eat?' Bethany changed the subject and when he named a restaurant which was as famous for its inflated prices as it was for the quality of its fare she gazed down at her jeans with dismay. Lesson one in how the super-rich operate. With a complete disregard for social convention. Cristiano clearly couldn't care less whether she was dressed for an expensive night out or not. He, himself, was casually attired in a pair of dark trousers and a white shirt which would have looked average on any other man on the planet but which looked ridiculously sexy on him.

'I'd rather not go there in a pair of jeans, flat shoes and a wrap,' Bethany told him tersely. She also suspected that walking into a place like that on the arm of a man like him would make her the cynosure of all eyes and she had never enjoyed basking in the limelight, particularly now, when the limelight would have a very dubious tinge. And what if he introduced her to someone? The rarefied world of the rich and famous was notoriously small. In Rome, it was probably the size of a tennis ball. She would be revealed for the imposter she was in seconds flat.

'You look…charming.'

'Not charming enough to go to that particular restaurant.' Bethany was feverishly cursing herself, yet again, for having succumbed to his invitation to dinner.

'Don't worry. I know the owner. Believe me when I tell you that he won't mind if I bring along a woman dressed in a bin bag.'

'Because you can get away with something doesn't give

you the right to go ahead and do it,' Bethany said, making sense to herself though not to him if his expression of bemusement was anything to go by.

'Why not?'

'Because it's important to have respect for other people,' she told him, repeating the oft held mantra with which she and her sisters had grown up.

Cristiano was looking at her as though she was slowly mutating into a being from another planet and Bethany blushed uncomfortably. She was well aware that she was probably in the process of contravening yet another unspoken dictum of the unbelievably rich, namely that she shouldn't be blushing like a kid.

'A socialite with principles,' he murmured with a slashing smile that made her breath catch in her throat and put paid to all her niggling qualms about what she was doing. 'I like it. It's rare in my world to meet a woman who's prepared to be vocal about her beliefs...' In truth, the women he went out with generally didn't give a hoot about what happened outside their own orbits. They were rich, had led, for the most part, pampered lives and their birthright was to accept the adulation of males and the subservience of everyone else.

Not that they would ever have dreamt of setting one foot into Chez Nico unless they were dressed to kill. In actual fact, he doubted whether very many would have dreamt of going anywhere unless dressed to kill because appearance was all.

'I'm not a socialite,' Bethany said uncomfortably.

'No? You just own a monstrously big apartment in the centre of Rome which you use as a holiday pad. You do fund-raisers. You're under thirty. Hate to tell you this, but that pretty much qualifies you as a socialite.'

'I told you, things don't work quite that way in…um…
where I come from.'

'And where's that?'

'Oh, you wouldn't have heard of it,' Bethany told him
truthfully. 'It's a little place in Ireland…um…in the middle
of nowhere…'

'A little place with a large ancestral manor house, by
any chance?'

'Yes, there's a large ancestral manor house…' Years
ago, she could remember her mother doing a cleaning stint
there to get some extra cash for Christmas. It was a great
grey mansion with turrets and a forbidding, desolate appearance.

'So you must be half Italian… Which half?'

Bethany gave a self-conscious laugh. 'Are you always
so interested in dinner companions you ask out on the spur
of the moment?'

'No. But, then again, I don't usually have to drag information out of my dinner companions. It's a fact that
most women love nothing more than talking about themselves.'

'You mean they try to impress you.'

'Do you want the truth or shall I treat you to a phoney
spectacle of false modesty?'

'You have a very big ego, don't you?'

'I prefer to call it a keen sense of reality.' Cristiano was
enjoying this banter. He had had to work to get her to this
place, on a date with him and, having got her here, was
discovering her to be skittish and unpredictable company.
It made a change from the doe-eyed beauties who were
always eager to oblige his every whim. 'Don't you feel the
need to impress me?' he murmured, his words cloaked in a
languorous, sexy intimacy that sent shivers racing up and
down her spine.

'Why should I?' A frisson of danger rippled through her. This was no simple, exciting night out with a stranger. She felt as though he was walking round her soul, opening doors she hadn't known existed.

'Because I feel the weirdest desire to impress *you*.' He also had the weirdest desire to find out more about her. Weird because *getting to know her* had not been remotely on the agenda when he had asked her out to dinner. He had seen her, had been curiously attracted to her, had thought nothing of entertaining himself with a one-night stand. It wasn't usually his scene but, then again, he would have been a complete hypocrite if he had tried to dredge up a bunch of reasons why he should not indulge in a night of passion with a woman he would probably never see again. It wasn't as though his goal in life, thus far, was to recruit a love interest for a permanent place in his life.

'Why don't you tell me what it would take…?'

His voice was like a caress, as was the lazy, amused, speculative expression in his eyes, although she noticed that he was keeping his distance, half leaning against the door, his long legs eating into the free space between them. She had not started the evening in the anticipation that it would end up in bed and had he tried to invade her space she would have pulled back at a rate of knots, but there was something wildly erotic about his self-restraint. It was a sobering thought to know that he would probably be repelled had he known her modest background. He might consider himself a man of the world, and he undoubtedly *was* a man of the world, a sleek, highly groomed, fantastically sophisticated animal who was the master of all he surveyed. Except there was quite a bit that he *didn't* survey, wasn't there?

'We could walk…' she said. 'Rome is full of so many exciting, wonderful sights. And then we could go somewhere simple and cheerful to eat. A pizzeria. I happen to know an excellent one not a million miles away from the Colosseum.'

'Sure. Why not? I haven't eaten in that part of the city since I was a teenager. In fact, I think I know the place you're talking about. Red and white striped awning outside? Dark interior? Empty wine bottles on the tables with candles, sixties style? Overweight proprietor with a handlebar moustache?'

'He must have lost weight over the years—' Bethany laughed '—but the moustache is still there. You used to go there? With your friends?'

'Before real life took over,' Cristiano said wryly.

'What do you mean by *real life*?'

'University and then stepping into my father's shoes. Pizzerias don't have much of a role to play in the life of an empire-builder.' He grinned, enjoying her forthright manner. It was refreshing to meet a woman so upfront. Those games women played could get a little tiresome after a while.

'So now you only go to fancy restaurants.'

'Where pizza is never on the menu.'

'Poor Cristiano.' Bethany laughed and their eyes tangled. She felt a rush of blood to her head because she could sense the sexual invitation in his slumberous, amused dark gaze.

'I know—' he sighed piteously, his eyes never leaving her face for a second '—condemned to a life without pizzas. No wonder you feel sorry for me. Okay, here's the deal. I'll do the pizza but I'll pass on the scenic walking. Enrico is paid far too much, as I keep telling him. What's the point of paying someone for doing nothing?'

'Who's Enrico?'

'My mother's driver, of course. Don't tell me you don't have one in London.'

'Several,' Bethany said, thinking of the numerous bus drivers who serviced the buses between her flat and the university.

'Good. Then that's settled.'

Bethany felt like a princess as she slid into the back seat of the sleek black Mercedes. A princess whose clothes didn't quite match the luxurious leather and gleaming walnut of the car, but what the heck? She had to restrain herself from running her hands along the seat. Presumably she would be accustomed to these levels of mega-luxury.

Seen from this angle, through the windows of a car that drew glances and had people swivelling around to try and glimpse who was inside, the city felt like her possession. No wonder that sense of *ownership* sat on this man's shoulders like an invisible mantle! Fifteen minutes in his car and she was already beginning to feel like royalty!

Even when they were installed at a table at the back of the buzzing, lively pizzeria, she was still hyper-sensitive to the reality that women were still sneaking sidelong glances at them, trying to figure out who the sexy guy was and his much drabber companion. Cristiano appeared to notice none of it.

He was busily delivering his verdict on the lack of changes to the pizzeria since he had last been there, which was nearly two decades ago, and she contented herself with arguing with everything he said, finally concluding that he was a snob for daring to inform her that the least the proprietor could have done was change the dated gingham tablecloths which loudly proclaimed a stubborn refusal to move with the times.

'Me? *A snob*?' He had been pleasantly invigorated by her arguing, because women didn't argue with him, and was now vastly amused at her one word summary of his character. She was laughing when she said it, her crystal clear green eyes throwing out all sorts of invitations that had him aching for her.

'Yes, you!' A bottle of wine had been brought for them and she had already finished one glass. 'Loads of people flock to this place because the food is simple and hearty and very, very good…'

'And would be improved by a shake up in the decor…'

'*You* like white linen and fawning waiters, but that doesn't mean that *everyone* shares your taste…'

'But most would, given half the chance.'

'*I* happen to prefer the rustic ambience…'

'How rustic? I'm sure I recognise a couple of those wine bottles stuffed with candles from when I was last here a hundred years ago.'

'I'm having dinner with an old man!' Bethany groaned in mock despair while he refilled her glass with some more wine and grinned in open appreciation of her teasing.

'You'd be surprised at what this old man is still capable of doing,' Cristiano intoned softly, the smile still playing on his lips as he savoured her flushed face with indolent thoroughness.

'Such as…?' Bethany questioned breathlessly. Her skin prickled and she felt quite unlike herself, as if she had stepped into another life, one where the normal rules of behaviour didn't apply. Which, she admitted to herself, she had. Kind of.

'Oh, running a business empire that has branches in most major cities in the world. Takes a lot of stamina to do that. Then there are my sporting interests. The usual gym routine, not to mention skiing, polo and very vigorous games of squash once a week.'

'Yes, that *is* impressive for a geriatric…' she said nonchalantly—at least she was aiming for nonchalance; inside, she was anything but as she experienced a sexual longing she had never felt before with any man. Nor had she ever indulged in sexual banter before. In fact, she had never indulged in sexual *anything*—at least nothing beyond kissing and the occasional groping. She had never seen the point of tossing her virginity out of the window for no better reason than because *everyone else her age had done it*. The temptation to do so now, with this man, curled inside her and made her feel as if she was no longer in complete possession of her own body.

'Then there's the sex…' His eyes never left hers. 'I've never had any complaints…'

'Aargh…' Colour flamed into her cheeks and she nervously grabbed her glass of wine and downed the contents. 'We were talking about the fact that you're a snob…' she reminded him shakily and he lowered his eyes, obliging her with a tactical retreat.

'And I was protesting my innocence of any such thing. A less snobbish person it would be hard to find!' he declared.

Bethany's nervous system settled a little now that she wasn't skewered by the naked hunger in his fabulous eyes, which he had made no attempt to conceal.

'Okay. So do you ever go *anywhere* inexpensive to eat?'

'You mean like one of those disgusting fast food places where people eat reconstituted meat drowning in sauce? No.'

'Cinema?'

Cristiano frowned. 'Not recently,' he admitted, surprised to find that it had been literally years since he had been inside one. Surely the last time couldn't have been at university?

'But you *do* go to the theatre? The opera?'

'Okay.' He held both hands up in surrender. 'I'm a crashing snob.' Their food had been brought to them and he hadn't even noticed. Nor had she. In fact, although the big bowl of pasta smelled amazing, the food still seemed like an unwelcome intrusion into a conversation that was unexpectedly energising.

'But, on a serious note—' he tucked in to the spaghetti, which was nothing like the dainty little portions served in expensive restaurants, usually as an accompaniment to the main dish, but a massively generous helping liberally covered in the finest seafood sauce he had tasted in a long time '—are you telling me that it isn't easy for you to be a feisty left wing radical when you have the comfort of money to support your ideals?'

'What do you mean?' For a second there, Bethany had almost forgotten the charade she was meant to be playing. She was reminded of it soon enough when he began to expound.

'Well, it's easy to relish the role of the free spirit, not tied to the shallow world of the rich and privileged, when you must know, at the back of your mind, that you could move between the two any time you wanted to. Yes, you come to pizzerias like this but, if you get a little bored, then it's well within your means to jump into a taxi and head for the nearest Michelin starred restaurant. And let's not forget the little matter of your apartment. Money can buy you the luxury of pretending to be one of the normal little people without any of the reality that goes with it.'

Bethany opened her mouth to contradict him and closed it just as fast. She could understand the irony of his observation and was powerless to refute it given the circumstances, so she made do with saying lamely, 'I'm not a left wing radical. Believe me.'

'And I'm not a snob. Believe me.' He gave her one of those toe-curling smiles that made her tummy flip over. 'Good food.' He raised his fork in appreciative acknowledgement. 'I might very well come back here again.'

'Are you sure the type of women you date would be up for this sort of place?' She found that she didn't care for the thought of him returning to her favourite haunt in the company of another woman. One of the leggy, glamorous brunettes with the dyed hair which he had previously mentioned. In fact, one of those women to whom he was much more suited, if only he knew it.

'Maybe not,' Cristiano conceded. 'Which makes you so unique.'

'Hardly. You should see this place some evenings. There's a queue a mile long to get inside. If I'm unique, then so are the hundreds of people who flock here every day of the year.'

'You know what I'm talking about.'

She did. 'You say that you're not a snob,' she heard herself say, 'but would you be sitting here opposite me if I weren't *unique*?'

'Meaning what?'

'Let's just say that I was…um…the genuine article. A pretty average girl from a working class background, just like all the girls in here…would you still be sitting where you are?'

It seemed a strange hypothesis but Cristiano was willing to go along for the ride because he had, quite frankly, never met anyone like her before. She was amazingly untouched by her wealth and if her conversation was unpredictable then it was just something else about her that he found so impossibly alluring.

Also, no one had ever raised the issue with him before and he frowned, giving her question thought.

'Probably not, if I'm to be honest.'

'Because…?'

'Because, like I said, a wealthy man can't be too careful. I would never allow myself to get tied up with a woman who wasn't financially independent in her own right. Marry in haste and repent at leisure and if you don't fancy doing the repentance bit, then you might just find yourself dragged through the courts and parting with a sizeable chunk of cash you've spent years working hard to attain. But hell, why waste valuable time talking about a situation that's not relevant?'

'I can't agree more,' Bethany agreed fervently because she had stepped into a princess's shoes and she wasn't going to spoil this one glittering night getting embroiled in an argument that was never going to go anywhere. She was Cinderella at the ball and why start beckoning to the pumpkin to come fetch her when it wasn't yet midnight?

He was entitled to his own opinions and he was entitled to protect his wealth however he saw fit, even if he *was* cutting himself off from so many experiences.

'So…' he kept his eyes on her while he beckoned to a waiter for the bill '…are we finished with the soul-searching conversations? Can we move on to something a little lighter? Or, failing that, why don't we just move on…?'

'To what? I don't know any clubs in Rome.' *And probably wouldn't have the cash to fund a visit even if I did.*

'I was thinking of somewhere a little…cosier. My place is less than ten minutes away.'

His scrutiny was hot and hungry and left her in no doubt that the outcome of the evening would finish in bed. *A one-night stand.* Her sisters would be shocked. Her parents would be mortified. Her friends would think that she had been taken over by an alien being who looked like her, spoke like her, but lived life in a different lane. Everything she took for granted about herself would be shattered and yet the pull to surrender to this new being was almost irresistible.

He made her feel sexy. Was making her feel sexy now, the way he was staring at her as if she were the only woman on the face of the planet. Her nipples nudged the white lace of her bra.

'Of course, I can just get Enrico to deliver you back to your apartment,' Cristiano told her, because he wasn't into forcing himself upon a reluctant woman, even if all the signals had been in place from the moment he'd picked her up from her apartment.

'Would you be very angry?'

'I would be in need of a very cold shower.'

Bethany had an image of him showering, his big, muscular body naked under the fine spray, his beautiful face raised, eyes closed, to the running water. It was an effort to keep her breathing even just thinking about it.

'Don't you want to get an early night?' she ventured tentatively and Cristiano laughed.

'I don't do early nights. I need very little sleep, as it happens.'

And that, in turn, made her think of them making love over and over, languishing on some great king-sized bed which probably had sheets of the finest, coolest Egyptian cotton and not the bargain basement stuff she was accustomed to. From calmly standing on the sidelines, she seemed to have morphed into a sexual creature in the space of a few hours. She had never had to fight off urges when it came to the opposite sex so it had been easy to put her celibacy down to her high-minded principles.

'Well…there's just one small thing…'

Cristiano could smell polite rejection in the making and, while he acknowledged that it would hardly be the end of the world, he was still surprised to find that his disappointment was much sharper than he had expected. But, then again, the evening had been much more pleasurable than he had anticipated. Usually, female conversation was a dullish background noise to which he paid lip service but essentially little in-depth attention. Tonight, he had found himself taking the time to really talk to her, to enjoy the unexpected pleasure of having a sparring partner who could make him laugh and pepper him with questions which had made him think.

'I'm all ears.' He settled the bill, brushing aside her offer to go Dutch, and sat back in the chair, giving her his full, undivided attention. The evening seemed to have been full of firsts, starting with the bizarre way he had invited her to dinner. Being turned down would also be a first.

'I…I'm not the most…um…you know….experienced person in the world…'

Cristiano sat forward, bewildered by this deviation from what he had been expecting. 'I don't get you.'

'What don't you get?' Bethany bristled defensively.

'I don't get what you're trying to tell me.'

'That's because you're not listening hard enough.' Embarrassment gave a sharp edge to her voice and she sighed. 'Okay. I know you have a certain idea of the person you think I am…' *expensive apartment in Rome, country house in Ireland, a string of drivers who presumably do nothing else but wait around in fancy cars for me to snap my fingers* '…but I'm not like all those other women you dated.' She took a deep breath and for a few seconds contemplated telling him the whole truth. The mix-up with the clothes, the silly little white lie…Would he laugh? Forgive her? No. The answer came before she could voice what was in her head. He would be horrified. He didn't go near girls like her, girls who didn't inhabit the same privileged background that he did. And she didn't want this moment with him to pass her by. She wasn't sure why she felt so strongly about it, but she did and she wasn't going to mess up her one snatched night with this guy. He had managed to crawl under her skin and she wanted him there.

'Here's the thing,' she said, spelling it out in black and white. 'I'm a virgin.'

CHAPTER THREE

'I'm a virgin...'

Possibly the only three truthful words she had uttered to him as she had played him for a complete and utter fool.

Cristiano, parked in a dark green Land Rover he had rented in Limerick, coldly surveyed his quarry, which was a picture postcard thatched cottage at the end of the road.

It was five months since she had walked out on him without warning and five weeks since he had discovered that she had strung him along with a pack of lies. Amelia Doni was no fresh-faced, copper-haired girl with green eyes and a knack for teasing him that had proved so addictive that he had cancelled his return to London and ended up whisking her off in his private jet to Barbados for two weeks. Amelia Doni, when he'd accidentally bumped into her over Christmas at his mother's house, was a blonde in her forties who, she'd told him in mind-numbing detail, had been on an extended cruise because she was recovering from a broken heart. She was the epitome of the wealthy owner of a slice of Rome's most prestigious apartment block and had bored him to death within two minutes. She had also stoked the fires of his simmering anger into a conflagration when he'd learned about her house-sitting arrangement with her darkly beautiful Italian god-daughter and realised the woman he had met had been an imposter.

Not only had he been summarily dumped, he had also been well and truly taken on a scenic route up a very winding garden path.

It had taken him a mere week to track down the address of one Bethany Maguire, and a couple more had passed as he sat on the information, telling himself to let it go before finally realising that he wouldn't rest until he had confronted the woman and given voice to his consuming rage.

He had no idea what he hoped to gain by confronting her and it went absolutely and utterly against the grain of the person he was, a man who had always been able to keep his emotions in check with ease, a man who prided himself on his ferocious self-control. A man, it had to be said, who had never found himself in the position of being left high and dry by any woman or, for that matter, being told barefaced lies and gullibly eating them up.

Without the engine running, it was beginning to get cold in the car and the January light was beginning to fade. Give it ten more minutes and the line of picturesque thatched houses that jostled for space along the broad road with colourfully painted cottages and shop fronts would fade into an indistinct grey blur. There was still time, he knew, to drive right back to the hotel, grab a meal and head back to London first thing in the morning. On the other hand, would that put paid to the bitter, toxic knot that sat in the pit of his stomach like a tumour?

He stepped out of the car and began walking along the pavement, cursorily taking in the fairy tale village setting. Not to his taste. The place looked as though it had been designed by a kid who had been given a blank canvas and told to go mad. He almost expected to bump into a ginger-bread house at any moment.

The house at the end of the road was no exception.

The trees were bare of leaves and the front garden lacked colour, but he imagined that in summer it would be filled with all the stereotypical stuff straight out of a children's book. Apple trees out back, flowers running rampant everywhere, the prerequisite stone wall over which neighbours would chat while, presumably, hanging out their washing and whistling a merry tune. He scowled and banked down the rise of bile in his throat as he ignored the doorbell to bang heavily on the front door instead.

Bethany, in the middle of foraging in the fridge for ingredients to make a meal for her parents which she had enthusiastically promised three hours earlier, cursed under her breath because she had left everything to the absolute last minute and couldn't afford to take time out for a chat. Having spent the past two years in London, she had forgotten how life worked in the small village where she had lived all her life. People stopped by. They chatted. They drank interminable cups of tea. It had been worse in the first couple of months after she had arrived back but, even now, old neighbours would drop in and would be offended if she didn't sit and chat over tea and biscuits.

She wondered if she could pretend to be out, perhaps duck down under the kitchen table and wait until the coast was clear, but then dismissed the idea because half the village would know that her parents were at the village fund-raiser and would also know that she had skipped it because she had felt ill that morning. That was just life around here, and she was going to have to make the best of it for the foreseeable future.

She dumped her handful of random ingredients on the kitchen counter and raced to the front door to intercept another bang.

In her head, she played over the possibilities of who it could be. Several of her old school friends, ones who had never left the little village in which they had grown up, who had settled down at ridiculously young ages to marry and have families, had looked her up. She had been grateful for their support and had tried very hard not to feel hemmed in and claustrophobic. She missed Shania and Melanie, who had both returned to their respective lives in Dublin after a two week family break over Christmas. Perhaps it was old Mrs Kelly a few houses along, who had become a frequent visitor and was prone to extended visits.

Bethany stifled a groan of near despair as she pulled open the front door and then stared at her visitor in frozen, nauseating disbelief.

She blinked, thinking that she must be hallucinating, but when she opened her eyes he was still there and this was no crazy illusion.

'*You!*' she squeaked in a high-pitched voice which she hardly recognised as her own. 'What are *you doing here?*' She clutched her mouth and swayed.

'No way are you going to faint on me,' Cristiano said through gritted teeth. He insinuated his foot over the threshold and pushed the door open wide, letting himself in while she was still gasping in shock and as pliable as a rag doll. Her eyes were as wide as saucers and she looked as though she was on the verge of collapse. Good.

Bethany heard the slam of the front door as he closed it and it resonated with the sound of the executioner's blade. She was busy trying to get her thoughts together but the sight of him, all six foot two of cold aggression towering in the hallway, had slowed her thought processes down to an unhelpful standstill.

'Cristiano,' she finally threaded unevenly. 'What a surprise.' Only the wall, against which she had pressed herself, was keeping her from sinking to the ground in an unlovely heap.

'Life is full of them. As I've discovered for myself, first-hand.'

'What are you doing here?' she stammered, choosing not to pursue that particular avenue of conversation.

'Oh, I was just driving by and I thought I'd take time out to pass the time of day with you…*Amelia*. But it's not Amelia, is it, *Bethany*?'

'I feel faint. I honestly do.' She put her hand to her head and took a few deep breaths. 'I think I'm going to be sick.'

'Feel free. I'll be waiting right here for you when you've recovered.' He closed the gap between them and with each passing step Bethany felt her heart rate rocket.

'How did…did you f…find me?'

'Now, now,' Cristiano said with sibilant menace, 'isn't it a little rude for you not to have offered me a cup of coffee? For us to be standing here in a hallway playing catch up when we could be chatting over old times somewhere a little more comfortable…? And after I've travelled all this way to see you…'

The man was in no hurry to go. And he was stifling her by standing so close, sending her frayed nervous system into even more acute disarray.

Belatedly, she remembered that she might be in the house on her own *at the moment* but her parents would be returning in under an hour, by which time he would need to have disappeared. The longer she remained in a state of shock, the longer he would be around, and she just couldn't afford to have him meet her parents.

Another wave of nausea threatened to have her rushing to the bathroom, but she quelled it and cleared her throat.

'Okay. I'll get you a cup of coffee, but if you've come

to bludgeon me into saying sorry then I'll spare you the effort. I'm sorry. Satisfied?'

'Not by a long chalk. So why don't we start with the coffee and then we can have a really good chat about everything. By the way, did you know that impersonating someone can be prosecuted as a criminal offence?'

Bethany paled and Cristiano, who had only thought of that on the spur of the moment, shot her a smile of pure threat.

'What else did you get up to while you were staying at the Doni apartment? Aside from shamelessly raiding her wardrobe? How light were your fingers? If I recall, the place was stuffed full of valuables.'

'How dare you?'

'I know. Nasty of me, isn't it? But I'd think twice before I start reaching for the moral high ground if I were you.' He had expected her to be taken aback by his appearance on her doorstep. No, he thought, scratch that. He had expected her to be shocked and defensive, but he hadn't bargained on the panicky apprehension in her eyes. Then again, she was a lady of unexpected responses and definitely not one whose words and actions could be taken at face value.

Bethany felt like a mouse pinned to the ground by a predator whose aim was to smack her around for a while before ripping her to shreds. When she had walked away from him, admittedly with a finality which stemmed more from cowardice than anything else, the last thing she had expected was to be hunted down. She hadn't taken him for a man who would lower himself to chasing after a woman who had dumped him without explanation. His pride would have seen to that. Unfortunately, she hadn't thought ahead to what he might do if he discovered that the woman who had dumped him had also been as genuine as a three pound note. At least as far as outward appearances went. Now she knew. He went on the attack.

'I wasn't trying to reach for any moral high ground.' Bethany shifted, crablike, against the wall because he was so close to her that she could feel his warm, angry breath on her face. 'I was just trying to say that I'm *not a thief*.'

'Now, I wonder why I'm finding it hard to believe anything you have to say…'

Since there was no arguing with that and trying to plead her innocence on that front was just going to be met with scathing disbelief, she decided that it was time for the cup of coffee. She deserved his anger and she would sit through it with lowered head and genuine repentance. Then he would leave and her life could return to its hollow routine.

'The coffee…I'll make you a cup…if…if you want to wait in the sitting room…it's just through there…'

'And have you out of my sight? Not a chance. I don't know whether you'll do a disappearing act through the back window. You seem to be pretty good at that.'

'I'm…sorry. I told you that.' She stared down at the ground but there was no escaping his presence because she could see the dull burnished leather of his shoes. Even when he stepped away to fall in behind her, she was horribly, horribly aware of him and it felt as though she was holding her body in agonising tension just to stop herself from shaking like a leaf in a high wind.

'Nice house,' he said conversationally, which didn't fool her for a minute into thinking that he had dropped his anger in favour of a more reasonable approach to having his questions answered. He was just enjoying the moment, toying with her. 'Funny, you told me that you lived in London.'

'I did.' She had her back to him as she filled the kettle with water and fetched down one of the mugs from the mug tree by the sink. Sadly, she couldn't take refuge in the task of making his coffee for ever and eventually she was obliged to turn around, albeit reluctantly, to find that he had taken up residence on one of the pine chairs at the kitchen table. It was a reasonably big kitchen, big enough to fit a generously proportioned table, but he still managed to reduce the space to the size of a prison cell.

She shoved the mug of coffee in front of him and sat on the chair furthest away. This cold-eyed stranger staring at her with biting antagonism was as far away from the sexy, amusing, highly intelligent charmer who had swept her off her feet sufficiently for her to extend her *one night of fun* into a two week, mind-blowingly idyllic trip to paradise as chalk was from cheese.

Playing at the back of her mind was his casual insinuation that she could be prosecuted for impersonation. Was that true? Could that really happen? She couldn't even begin thinking about that, so she shut the horror of it away and focused instead on the humiliation awaiting her at his hands.

Of course she deserved it. She had meant so many times to confess the truth to him, but every time she'd got to within striking distance of doing so she had pulled back because she hadn't wanted their affair to end. Instead, she had laughingly sidestepped awkward questions, glazed over the truth and generally done such a good job of dancing round anything remotely incriminating that she could have had a career as an escape artiste. Houdini would have been proud of her.

In the process, he had stolen her heart and if he had asked her to stay on in sunny Barbados for another fortnight she knew she would have jumped at the chance and postponed the inevitable again.

Her punishment was as deadly as it was conclusive. He

had taken up residence inside her and not a single day had gone by when she hadn't thought about him and about the fact that she would never be entitled to have him in her life again. Ever.

'Stop looking at me like that,' she muttered mutinously.

'Like what? How do you expect me to look at a liar, a cheat and a thief?'

'I told you *I didn't steal anything from Amelia Doni!*'

'But you certainly managed to rip me off for quite a bit when you count the dinners, the wardrobe, the first class ticket to the other side of the world...'

'You don't understand...'

'Enlighten me.' He sat forward and Bethany instinctively cringed back, licking her lips nervously, with one eye on the clock behind him over the kitchen door.

'I meant to tell you the truth...'

'The road to hell is paved with good intentions.' He intoned the age-old motto with icy grimness. 'When did the good intentions disappear? When you realised that it would be a hell of a lot more rewarding to hop on the gravy train and take advantage of my generosity? Sex with all expenses paid?'

'Don't be crude!'

'When did you decide to leave London?'

'Wha...?' Confused by the abrupt change of subject, Bethany looked at him in bewilderment before her brain clanked back into gear and she caught on to what he was doing. Instead of going for the kill, he was nipping away at her, pulling back before he could draw blood, only to home back in again just when she had managed to recover. He was getting under her defences and making sure that she had no time to rebuild them.

'London. When did you decide to leave? Ditch the university course? Fly back over here, to the middle of no-where? Did you think that London was too small for the both of us? Was your conscience acting up too much for you to stay put and risk running into me at some unspeci-fied point in time?'

Bethany paled as his carelessly tossed question found its unintentional target.

'How…how did you find me, Cristiano?' She fell back on her original query. 'And why did you bother?'

Cristiano shrugged elegantly. Even at the height of his anger, when his face was a cold mask of freezing disdain, she couldn't help but register his magnetic pull. Everything about him was unbearably graceful, unbearably and un-fairly masculine, and her memory had not begun to do justice to his shamefully abundant sex appeal. She was ashamed to find that she was lapping it up, shoving it into some storage compartment in her brain from whence she knew she would retrieve it over and over again in the future. The man who had once told her that he had never felt what she made him feel with any other woman now loathed her and still she was helplessly feeding off his beauty like a brainless leech.

'Why did I bother?' Cristiano drawled in a voice that sent shivers running up and down her spine. 'Good ques-tion. I didn't. You might have done a midnight flit but, hell, I'm man enough to cope with a bit of dented pride…' It felt good to let her know straight off the bat that she had left no lasting impact on him whatsoever. Okay, so the image of her had been annoyingly intrusive, had made him lose concentration in the occasional meeting, but he would have stuck it out and he was sure he would have forgotten about her in a couple of months. And if he had felt no inclina-tion to look at another woman since her, then that made sense. In fact, it pointed to a certain amount of wisdom because only a fool would have jumped back into the water so soon after having been attacked by a shark. 'Easy come, easy go,' he additionally pointed out. 'But now, here's the thing… There's a difference between a woman walking out and a woman who's played me for a fool.'

Bethany greeted this with silence because she had said sorry enough to make her realise that apologies weren't denting his implacable anger.

Another thought crept into her fevered mind and took root. What if he had come for more than just an explanation? What if he had come to recover all the money he had spent on her? Yes, there were the meals and then the wardrobe. She had taken over her own clothes, claiming to have shoved things into a suitcase at the very last minute because the trip to Barbados had been so unexpected. This had left her in the awkward position of arriving at his spectacular beach house without a swimsuit to her name and when he had offered to go on a shopping trip with her she had guiltily agreed and only half-heartedly offered to pay.

Sex with all expenses paid. His words reverberated in her head like acid and made her feel cheaper than a common tart. Of course she had bagged up all the clothes the minute she had returned to London and given the lot to charity, but she doubted he would believe that and how could she protest her innocence in that small, insignificant matter when she was so palpably guilty of a much larger fraud? Regret attacked her on all fronts.

Then there was the small matter of those flights. First class. She had no idea how much that ran to but she knew it wouldn't be hundreds.

She paled at the thought of how much she would owe him. God, she hadn't even got a job yet. In two weeks' time she would be starting work at the local school, covering for someone on maternity leave, but that would be nowhere near the kind of money she would need. The cash register in her head pinged with such force that she buried her face in her hands and emitted a soft moan of pure despair.

'Yes, I know,' Cristiano said without a trace of sympathy. 'Our sins usually *do* end up catching up with us.'

'I don't understand how you knew where I lived…'

'Because you made sure to keep it a secret? I happened to meet the *real* Amelia Doni at my mother's house. Imagine my surprise when I discovered that she was a forty-something blonde with an axe to grind about the male sex.'

'What did you tell her?' Bethany immediately thought of Amy and her hapless friend who was now on the road to recovery. She looked at him, wide-eyed and nervous.

'Nothing. Of course. I explain myself to no one. I did manage to find out, however, who *should* have been house-sitting and it was just a matter of time before I got my people to link the connections and find out the person at the end of the chain.'

'*Your people?*'

'You'd be surprised at how efficient they can be at finding me the answers I need. Like bloodhounds.'

'Amy asked me to house-sit,' Bethany told him immediately. 'Catrina had asked her because she was over in London…'

'In rehab. Yes, I know.'

'She didn't want her godmother to find out. Look, there was no harm in anything we did.'

'Do you really think I give a damn about some dippy girl with an addiction?'

'No, but I'm just trying to tell you that…well…'

'Let's cut to the chase, shall we? When I showed up at the apartment, why didn't you tell me immediately who you were…?'

Her subterfuge rose in his head like a mist of red rage as he remembered how conclusively he had been taken in by her, like a gullible teenager falling for the prom queen who told him that he was the centre of her world while fooling around with a hundred other guys.

'You caught me at a bad time...' Bethany whispered miserably. 'I was...I was...'

'Let me help you here. Playing at being the lady of the manor? In borrowed garb? Faking it?'

'Don't!'

'Don't *what*? Oh, yes, I forgot you had a problem with the truth.'

'I...Okay, I had been out in the sun, I had come back to the apartment and had a really long bath and I thought it might be fun to try on one of the dresses in the wardrobe. I've never owned anything expensive. I was tempted. Haven't *you* ever been tempted to do something you know you shouldn't?'

'Strangely enough, I have some notion of the difference between right and wrong!'

'It didn't seem *wrong* at the time!'

'No? So tell me...*when* did it start *seeming wrong*? Or didn't it?'

'I wasn't expecting anyone to come by,' Bethany muttered. 'And then you invited yourself in...'

'Don't even *think* of trying to palm off the blame for your deception onto me!'

'I wasn't!' Bethany backtracked hurriedly. A glance at the kitchen clock told her that although, over the past few months, time had seemed to go by at a numbingly slow pace, it was now speeding past.

'Going somewhere?' Cristiano drawled, not missing a thing. 'Hot new date with some hapless guy who thinks you're someone you're not?'

Bethany clasped her dampened hands together and ignored the thickly sarcastic interruption. 'I was just trying to explain…you came in and I couldn't very well start babbling about trying on someone else's clothes. I wasn't even *supposed* to be in the apartment in the first place! I didn't want to land my friend Amy in trouble and I don't know Catrina, but I gathered that finding out she was in rehab would have blown her relationship with her godmother out of the sky…'

'So, because you're such a *thoughtful* and *considerate* human being, you thought it wise to keep mum…'

'I never expected that things would end up where they did,' Bethany said in a burst of defensiveness. Another five minutes had been gobbled up since she had last looked at the clock. And he'd only taken a couple of sips of the coffee which he had made a point of demanding!

'You mean…*in bed*…?'

'Yes!'

'By which time, it naturally didn't occur to you that I might have been entitled to learn the real identity of the woman I was sharing my bed with…'

'I wasn't putting on an act when I was with you.'

'Run that by me again?'

'I'm really sorry… You *were* entitled to know everything, but I was scared that…that…'

'That you might lose out on a *real* taste of the high life?'

'No! I'm not like that!'

'Forgive me if I'm struggling to think otherwise.'

'I was a…a virgin!' Bethany whispered shakily.

'Meaning…? What, exactly?' It angered him that all his logical thought processes were veering away from the stark black and white attack and shame route he had envisaged. She was a scheming, lying bitch but she was still managing to get under his skin with her wobbly voice and her shaking hands. 'Is your virginity supposed to be a blanket excuse for the fact that you lied to me for two weeks? Maybe the simple truth is that trading in your virginity for fun and frolics with a wealthy man seemed like a pretty good exchange.'

'You don't know me at all if you can say that!'

'Events would seem to suggest otherwise. Why didn't you just come clean when the holiday was finished?' Cristiano demanded. 'Why do the vanishing act?'

Bethany opened and shut her mouth. How could she tell him that she might have confessed everything if he had been the simple fling that she had anticipated? If she had been capable of walking away and relegating him to the role of some amusing escapade which didn't have the ability to touch her, she might have come clean because his reaction wouldn't have mattered to her, not really. But she had fallen in love and his reaction *would* have mattered. Either way, she would have been walking away but she just hadn't been able to face walking away with the image of his shock and hatred in her head. How on earth would she ever have been able to rid herself of it?

So instead she had done the midnight flit. Literally. They had returned to Italy and, over their last meal, back to the pizzeria where they had had their first, he had held her hand across the table, playing with her fingers, threatening that he would be looking her up in London and then later, after he had returned to his own place, she had quietly packed up her paltry belongings—she couldn't really stay as Amy had reluctantly returned to take up her house-sitting duties when Bethany had taken a leaf out of her book and flitted off to Barbados—and she had left. It had been pretty close to midnight, as it happened.

'I should have left a note,' Bethany now said miserably. 'I should have explained everything in a note.'

Cristiano felt a surge of anger. 'Because, of course, telling me to my face would have been just a little too much like hard work,' he said scathingly, and she flinched.

'I knew how you'd react. Like this.'

'Tell me. I'm curious. How much of your personality did you have to edit to accommodate your charade?'

'I didn't edit *any* of my personality!'

'You just fine-tuned it to fit in with the deceit.'

'No!'

'So you really *are*…sweet, genuine, easy to laugh… Hmm, finding it a tad tricky to believe that…'

'Oh, this isn't getting either of us anywhere.' She stood up and swept her hands across her forehead wearily. The ingredients for the promised dinner lay forgotten on the counter top. 'It was all a terrible mistake and I can't say much more than *I'm sorry* and I understand why you're angry with me.' A tear threatened to squeeze itself out and she pressed her fingers against her eyes, sending it right back from whence it was trying to come.

This was a nightmare. She had never expected him to descend on her in the one small corner of the planet where she had taken refuge.

'Why do you keep looking at the clock?' Cristiano said suddenly. 'This is the fourth time in the past fifteen minutes.' He wondered if his crack earlier on about her having a hot date had been nearer the mark than he had intended. Never one to indulge in wild flights of imagination, and certainly never in connection with a woman, he now found himself gritting his teeth furiously together at the thought of her with a new plaything. Some local village lad who had doubtless been waiting in the wings for her to return. Someone who, at least, had the luxury of knowing the woman he was dealing with, instead of some fictitious person fabricated from a mixture of lies and play acting.

'Am I? I didn't think I was.'

'And who is the food for?' He jerked his head at the unprepossessing pile of vegetables. 'Entertaining? Is this why you jacked in the university course and hotfooted it back here? Does he know about us?'

'What are you talking about?' But there was a nervous stutter in her voice that sabotaged any attempt at sounding genuinely innocent of a hidden agenda and his eyes narrowed suspiciously on her face.

An ugly, insidious thought crept into his head like poison. Never lacking in the confidence stakes when it came to women, he wondered now whether his eager little virgin hadn't used him as an unsuspecting trial run for someone else. A rampant flare of jealousy forced aside the nonsensical idiocy of the supposition, leaving him with a series of graphic images of her offering her body for another man's pleasure.

'Now, I wonder what your local sweetheart would say about a woman who spends two weeks in another man's company and at another man's bidding...before hightailing it back home to him...? Hmm...? Not many men would be forgiving on that score. In fact, I would say roughly *none*. So have you told him about your overseas romp? Or were you using me so that you could take your newly found sexual experience into his bed?'

'Don't be ridiculous!' Bethany spluttered, her face scarlet as much from his far-fetched accusations as from the evocative pictures he was unwittingly creating in her head. Pictures of *them* together on *their* overseas romp. She had gone to him a virgin, but at the end of two weeks she had become a recklessly wanton woman who had had every inch of her body slowly and meticulously explored and had tasted the delight of exploring every inch of *his* body. In fact, there had not been a night since when she hadn't recreated those memories in her head.

'Am I being ridiculous? Why else would you have come back here? Left London and your university degree? If not for a man?'

The silence that greeted this question stretched between them like a piece of elastic being pulled to its absolute limit. 'Not everything a woman does is because of a man.' Bethany struggled to sound as normal and natural as she could, which was not very as her voice was a weak croak.

'But most of the time it is. At least, that's always been my experience.'

She resisted looking at the clock. Again. Although it was difficult.

'Okay, if you must know, I promised I'd cook something for my parents. They've gone to the village hall…some sort of do to raise money for an orphanage in Africa. They'll be back soon. I'm sure you don't want to be here when they arrive…'

He didn't leap from his seat. She didn't even know if he believed a word of what she had said. In any case, it didn't matter because the sound of the front door opening impacted like a bullet through her panicky thoughts and she heard her mother's familiar voice calling, 'Honey? Bethany? We're home!'

CHAPTER FOUR

For the space of a few desperate seconds Bethany wondered if she could reasonably hide Cristiano, who had risen to his feet and was adding to her feeling of suffocation. Stuff him away in a cupboard somewhere or else shove him into the back garden and lock the door on his harsh, beautiful face, now alive with curiosity.

The only upside was that at least she had proved him wrong on his fanciful idea that she was inviting some man back to the house.

She raced out to intercept her parents and found them in the act of removing their coats and making noises about the weather, which had apparently taken a turn for the worse. Snow predicted.

'But the fund-raiser was an enormous success.' Eileen Maguire smiled at her daughter. 'Raised well over five hundred euro. Doesn't sound like a lot, but every little helps. There was a very interesting chap there, Bethany. Gave a talk about where the money would be going. Wasn't he interesting, John? I was tempted to ask him back here for supper; poor man is having to make do with sandwiches at the B&B because Maura's gone to visit her daught…'

Her mother stopped in mid-sentence, which was a phenomenon that seldom occurred, and Bethany didn't have to look around to know why. She could *feel* Cristiano's presence in the hall behind her. Why on earth couldn't he have stayed in the kitchen just a tiny bit longer? Given her time to warn her parents of the unexpected arrival?

'Mum…Dad…' She turned round reluctantly as Cristiano moved smoothly towards her. So she hadn't been lying. There was no man hovering on the scene, as he had mistakenly suspected. At least not at this moment in time. He just couldn't figure out why all the drama when she could just have told him that her parents would be heading back. Would that have been his cue to leave? He wasn't sure. Having been reeled in by an expert liar, he might have been curious to meet her parents. As it stood, he could not have been in the company of two more normal people. Both appeared to be in their late fifties, possibly a bit older.

'I'm…'

'We know who you are, son, and I'm just glad we've finally met you. Aren't we, Eileen? She's glad too,' John Maguire said, smiling with his hand outstretched, 'and will tell you so herself just as soon as she stops gaping like a goldfish. Mind you…' he shook Cristiano's hand warmly and winked at his daughter, who was standing to one side, her face ablaze with hot colour '…perhaps we should relish seeing her lost for words. As Beth probably told you, it's a rare sight.'

Not, Bethany thought with an agonising sense of doom, as rare a sight as it was to witness Cristiano lost for words, which he clearly was and she couldn't blame him. Nor could she begin to imagine what was going through his head, although he seemed to gather his wits with insufferable speed, returning her father's handshake before moving on to, of all things, raise her mother's hand to his lips in a purely Italian gesture of chivalry, which had her mother blushing like a teenager.

'Oh, my,' she said, glancing over to Bethany. 'You said

that he was dashing, darling, but you didn't let on just how *much of the gentleman he was*!'

'Dashing?' Cristiano slanted a look across at her that might have seemed innocent enough to her gullible parents but was loaded with questions of a highly uncomfortable nature as far as Bethany was concerned.

'I'm afraid I didn't quite get round to making that meal…' Bethany changed the subject to a general chorus of *Never mind* and *We understand perfectly* from her parents.

'You should have called us, darling!' Eileen was smoothing down her grey skirt, moving forward to warmly take both of Cristiano's hands in hers. 'We would have hurried back! No. That wouldn't have been such a good idea, would it, John?' She glanced at her husband as though he had been the one to make the silly suggestion and he raised both his shoulders with an air of indulgent resignation. 'I guess you two young things had so much to catch up on! Now, Bethany, you stay here with Cristiano…*such* a lovely name…no, better still, why don't you take Cristiano into the sitting room…John, darling, will you get the fire going…? And…'

'Good idea, Mum!' No. There was no way that she could bear to face Cristiano.

'And don't you worry about the food, Beth…' John turned to the other man and grinned. 'I've told this young lady a thousand times that…'

'Dad! *Please*. I'm sure Cristiano doesn't want to hear all sorts of boring stuff…'

'Boring stuff? If there's one thing I've discovered about your daughter, John, it's that the word *boring* can never be applied to her. Can it, Bethany?' His voice was silky smooth and was it her imagination but did it also sound as menacing as the slash of a knife ripping through paper?

Or maybe, she thought with a sick feeling in her stomach, flesh. Hers.

'We'll just take ourselves off to the sitting room now and why don't you and Mum…er…go and change…and then we can…'

'Get to know one another!' Her father was beaming and Bethany smiled back weakly.

'And I'll just rustle up something for us all to eat. It'll have to be simple fare, mind…' She looked at Cristiano, who scored another few Brownie points by immediately offering to take them all out to dinner. Snow, he was told, was on the way. Best stay put.

'In that case, I couldn't want for anything nicer than a simple meal. Your daughter must have told you that I'm a man of uncomplicated tastes.'

That earned him a friendly pat on the shoulder from the older man who said, to Bethany's horror, although how much more horrible could the situation get? 'Guess that's the way it plays with the kind of risks you take on with what you do, eh?'

Cristiano greeted this bewildering statement with a non-committal smile and said nothing. His life, until he had met the woman hovering slightly behind him, had been an ordered affair. Work. Women. Everything in its place. He was a man who had always believed that by wielding firm control he could successfully limit unpleasant surprises and thus far he had never had occasion to doubt the philosophy. So he was ill prepared for the sensation of walking on quicksand, which was what he felt he was doing now. Risks? Sure, he took risks in his line of work, but somehow he had got the impression that the risks to which Bethany's father had referred did not apply to those associated with high finance, mergers and acquisitions. So what the hell had the man been talking about? And how, for that matter, had they known his identity before the usual round of introductions?

Behind him, Bethany cleared her throat and he spun around to face her as her parents disappeared up the stairs, talking in low, excited voices.

It grated on his nerves, but even in her own territory, a modest thatched cottage a million miles away from glamorous designer shops and sexy wine bars, she still had the look of a woman who could reel in any unsuspecting man with the pretence of being born to privilege. She didn't have the air of someone who looked down on anyone they considered their inferior, which was just one of the things he found so insanely irritating about many of the women he had dated in the past. Bethany, instead, just looked refined. Something about the way she was put together. Maybe the vibrant, rich colour of her hair tumbling down past her shoulders. Or the perfect clarity of her eyes. Or maybe it was the silky smoothness of her skin with its dusting of freckles, untouched by the make-up mask so many women used to camouflage less than flawless complexions. Or perhaps the manner in which she held herself. Poised, proud and assertive but in a very muted way.

Angry with himself for even bothering to register her as anything more than a woman who had had the temerity to play games with him, Cristiano looked at her with grim, unsmiling menace. As always, silence proved to be his ally and Bethany stumbled into speech, her eyes shifting away from his as she led him towards the sitting room. He listened without saying a word as she rambled on about her parents, apparently pillars of the community, involved in all sorts of charitable causes, virtual saints if her eulogy was anything to go by.

As he listened, he took in everything around him, from the profusion of family photos to the gleaming ornaments collected over a lifetime and obviously cherished. Although just a cottage, it was an extremely spacious one and the downstairs was comprised of a honeycomb of little rooms which quaintly interconnected with one another. On one of the chairs in a room which had been kitted out as a study, a fat, contented tabby cat was snoozing. This couldn't be further removed from the ancestral manor she had given him to believe was her family home and Cristiano hung on to the thought, which provided just the right spur for the aggression with which he had earlier confronted her.

'So,' he said conversationally, once they were in the sitting room and he was installed on one of the sprawling comfy chairs, 'what a charming place your parents have. So different from the turreted mansion you described...'

Bethany blushed. She hadn't been treated to Cristiano's brutally cold side, although she had known it was there because men of power were invariably ruthless, and she was finding it hard to marry the two personas. The gorgeous, sexy man who had whisked her away to a tropical idyll and the icy stranger looking at her with shuttered eyes and a cruel curl on his lips. She had to remind herself that she would never have glimpsed the gorgeous, sexy man if he had met her as Bethany Maguire. She might not have met the icy stranger, but she would bet her limited savings that Mr Indifferent would have been in ample supply.

'I never said that the turreted mansion belonged to my parents,' she told him. 'I only said that there was certainly one in my home town and there is.'

'I'm afraid I find it hard to appreciate the fine line of distinction between an outright lie and an economical use of the truth.'

'You're only finding it hard because you don't even want to try.'

'And why should I? But you were right when you said

that there was no point going over old ground. It's not going to get either of us anywhere. So let's move on to another topic, shall we?' He delivered an icy smile that sent flutters of real fear racing through her body. Cristiano, seeing that, broadened his smile and relaxed. He had wondered why he had bothered to make the trip but now he knew. Yes, he had needed to see her face to face so that he could exorcise some of his built up fury with her for lying to him and with himself for being taken in by her deception. He had also, he now realised, felt the urge to close what he considered unfinished business because what they had *was* unfinished.

The two weeks they had spent in Barbados had been tantamount to a complete, reckless breakdown of his self-control. He had been like a straight A student who had decided to play truant. Naturally, she had been blissfully unaware of that, had not known that that was the first time in his life when he had breached his own rigidly self-imposed boundaries. Cristiano wasn't quite sure how she had managed to achieve that feat but achieve it she had and, by the time they had returned to Italy, he was by no means ready for her to vanish from his life. Seeing her again here had had the negative effect of reminding him why he was still so damned hot for her. He had expected to feel nothing for her but derision and contempt. And sure, she was little more than a cheap liar, but the knowledge hadn't gone very far to extinguishing the flare of attraction he had neither sought nor courted but which was, it seemed, still there and very firmly alight.

Even looking at her now across the width of the sitting room, folded into the chair like a kid with the long sleeves of her oversized jumper pulled right down so that she could catch the ends between her slender fingers, was alternately rousing and enraging him.

Like a mathematician addressing a convoluted problem, Cristiano brought his finely tuned and coolly logical brain to bear on the illogical situation. How better to put an end to his anger and frustration than by just taking what had been summarily denied him? Could he *pretend* to overlook the little matter of her outrageous deception until he got her into bed and sated his hunger for her, which was still running through his veins and sabotaging all his efforts to get his life back on track?

He'd have to think about that one but he relaxed for the first time since he had set foot in the house. Just having a solution to hand, even if he decided not to put it to use, went some way to re-establishing his control over proceedings which, with the appearance of her parents, had taken a definite knock.

Also, he quite liked the nature of his solution. He hadn't been able to shake the memory of her face from his head, or the memory of her moaning under him, on top of him, in the massive circular bath at his house in Barbados, in the pool, in various parts of the house and several times on his private stretch of beach where only the moon and the stars had witnessed their inexhaustible passion. It would be sweet revenge, not that he applied such a primitive description to his wandering thoughts, to take her again and then leave her, but when the time was right and at his say-so.

He surfaced from his unexpectedly pleasant thoughts to see her perched forward on the edge of her chair, staring at him intently.

'Did you hear me?'

Cristiano frowned. 'Repeat,' he commanded. 'My mind was elsewhere.'

Bethany could only assume that having given her the full force of his fury he was already thinking about leaving, getting back to his wonderful, privileged life—the same wonderful, privileged life he had mistakenly assumed she knew all about.

And, God, she was so tempted to let him walk out of the door but then…how would she explain that to her parents? The web of deceit which she had begun weaving the minute she had accepted his dinner invitation all those months ago wrapped a little tighter around her.

She was also discovering that the thought of seeing him for the last time *again* was already beginning to dig its claws in. She mentally stuck that inappropriate reaction into a box in her head and firmly taped it down.

'I was *saying* that there are one or two things that I need to tell you before Mum and Dad come back down.'

Cristiano's antennae immediately went onto red alert.

'You mean aside from explaining how it is that your parents seemed to know who I was without any introductions having to be made?'

'I…um…told them about you.'

'Really. And what exactly did you say? I'm keen to know, considering your amazing capacity for stretching the truth.' His eyes drifted lazily from her flushed face down to her breasts—breasts which he had known intimately, had tasted and luxuriated in. It made no difference that they were well hidden under the capacious jumper. His memory was more than up to supplying an image of the luscious body beneath it.

Bethany's brain threatened to shut down. 'I told them… you know…that we met while I was out in Italy…'

'Oh, so they *knew* that you were in Italy. That's a promising start. Did they know that you were house-sitting for a random stranger whom you had decided to impersonate?'

'Yes, they knew that I was house-sitting!'

'Lose the pious tone, Bethany. It doesn't suit you. And

I take it that you didn't breathe a word about your charade of being one Ms Amelia Doni…? Hmm…?'

Bethany could feel the slight dampness of perspiration on the palms of her hands, but she kept them well covered in the sleeves of her jumper. 'No,' she admitted.

'Didn't think so. Your parents didn't strike me as the sort of people who would find it an amusing anecdote. So what exactly did you tell them about me?'

'Right. Okay.' Bethany cleared her throat and braced herself. 'I know you probably think it a bit peculiar that I would even mention you, considering things didn't exactly end well.'

'Understatement of the year, don't you think?'

'But they're very moral people. Great believers in the sanctity of relationships…'

'Obviously a trait that they didn't pass on to you, then.'

'You're not going to make this easy for me, are you?'

'Any reason why I should?'

'I just don't think that this is such a great time for us to be arguing.' Her eyes flicked towards the door but her parents were still safely upstairs. Knowing them as well as she did, they would be taking their time, giving her time to be alone with Cristiano. She felt faint when she thought about the length, breadth and width of her crazy deception.

'What have the moral values of your parents got to do with anything?' Cristiano suddenly asked. Astute at reading all situations, two and two in this case was not adding up to four. Even for Bethany, downright liar, possible thief, massive opportunist and altogether unpredictable entity, there were strands of her conversation that were just not adding up to anything he could catch hold of.

'Can I just say that I never, ever expected you to turn up

here out of the blue?' Bethany could feel her heart thudding in her chest as though it was about to explode. 'I mean you're a sophisticated guy. I guess I thought that you'd look back at what we had as nothing more than a pleasant interlude. I didn't think ahead how you would react if you ever found out about…you know…'

Cristiano could smell a dodge a mile off but he was willing to let the cross-examination ride because, sooner or later, she would get down to answering all the questions flying around in his head. The ones which she was ostensibly dancing around at the moment.

'Dashing.'

'I beg your pardon?'

'*Dashing*. Wasn't that the word your mother used to describe me?'

'Right. Yes. Dashing. And adventurous.'

'Dashing and *adventurous*?'

Bethany nodded miserably.

'Why am I beginning to find this all a little surreal?' He stood up and began pacing the room, pausing to look at the happy photos in frames on the mantelpiece, on the bookcase in the corner, on the small round table by the window. Here were parents who were immensely proud of their offspring. Within a five metre radius, a lifetime of joyful memories was played out in a succession of pictures.

'I know it must seem a bit crazy…'

'A *bit*?' He swung round to look at her, pinning her to the chair with an intensity that brought her out in goosebumps. She had thought it difficult dealing with the remembered version of Cristiano. She now knew that *difficult* took on a whole new meaning when it came to dealing with the real thing.

While she struggled to put her thoughts into order and find a way of explaining *the surreal situation*, Cristiano strolled over to her chair and then leaned down, supporting himself on the sides of her chair and instantly bringing every nerve in her body to attention.

His clean, masculine scent filled her nostrils and inflamed her senses and her eyes fluttered, riveted to his striking face. *Dashing* didn't even begin to do justice to his strikingly handsome, lean, bronzed face. Awash with fear and panic, she was still aware of her body reacting to his proximity, her nipples tightening with remembered pleasure and her mouth softening. She looked down quickly but not so quickly that Cristiano didn't see her unconscious reaction to him.

He felt a kick of satisfaction. So *something* had been real. She might have lied about everything under the sun because a trip to sunny Barbados had been just too good an opportunity to pass up, but she hadn't lied about wanting him. When she had fallen into his arms, it had been the real thing. Furthermore, if he still wanted her, and it was a big *if*, then she was his for the taking.

'So I'm dashing,' he prompted, his voice smooth and cool, 'and adventurous…'

'Could you please…stop looming over me?' Bethany squeaked in response, and Cristiano anchored himself even more firmly to her chair.

'Why? Does it make you feel uncomfortable? Does your guilty conscience bother you when I'm up this close and personal? Or maybe…' he felt a burst of savage, unwelcome desire as his libido went into overdrive '…you're terrified that what you really want is for your *dashing, adventurous* ex-lover to get even more up close and personal…' He was rewarded by a fleeting look in her eyes that gave him the answer he had already suspected. Satisfied, he stood up and sauntered back to his own chair. If this were a game, which it most definitely was not, he figured he had scored the first point.

'So…you were telling me why you had an insane desire to spill the beans about our little fling to your parents…'

This time it was Bethany's turn to stand up. She walked towards the door, which was slightly ajar, and shut it completely. Her parents would be tactfully keeping out of the way but sooner rather than later they would head down for a bit of family bonding and the last thing she needed was to have her conversation eavesdropped.

When she sat back down, it was on the sofa next to his chair, close enough to talk without having to raise her voice, even though her body was still humming from the dangerous thrill of being so close to him. She didn't want to dwell on the mortifying fact that he had seen right through her, deep down to the helpless longing she had felt then and now. Had he also seen how *bone deep* it was? Like a stubborn weed, it fought through everything, including his hostility, condemnation and glacial contempt. She could hardly blame him, given the circumstances, that he would use her own weakness for him against her. If he had tried to kiss her just then, she didn't think that she would have been able to resist. The fact that he had brought her to that point only to pull back would have satisfied just a bit of his wounded pride and dented ego and she tried very hard to look at it from his point of view. Fair was fair, after all.

Which didn't mean that she wasn't still smarting from his rejection.

'Yes. Right.'

'And, by the way, *how* adventurous am I? Exactly?'

Bethany drew in a shaky breath. 'You wouldn't believe,' she said.

'I'm surprised you wanted to paint a picture of our sex life with your parents,' Cristiano remarked sardonically.

'Sorry?'

'Well…' he shrugged, still on a high from having irrefutable proof that she was as hot for him as he was for her and from successfully exerting his will-power and turning her down '…if your parents are as moralistic as you tell me, then I'm a little surprised that you would discuss our sex life with them. Or was it more in the nature of a cosy mother and daughter chat?'

'Of course I haven't discussed our sex life with my mum! She'd be mortified!'

'Then what the hell are you talking about?'

'I'm talking about what you do!'

This time it was Cristiano's turn to look at her in pure bewilderment. Even for him, this was a leap too far. 'What do I do?'

'You make loads of money,' Bethany said feverishly. 'Running that empire of yours, but obviously that wasn't, you know, enough.'

'Wasn't it?' His clogged up brain was refusing to clear. He also didn't like the shifty way she was refusing to look him in the eye. She might have lied through her teeth the entire time they'd been together but she had never been one to avoid eye contact. She was avoiding it like crazy now.

'Well, no.' She sighed and a sense of inevitability gave her the courage to carry on in a more normal voice. 'You weren't satisfied building empires so you decided to embark on a programme of good deeds.'

'A *programme of good deeds*? Sorry, but you're losing me here.'

'I know. I guessed I might. And I know you're not going to like what you're about to hear, but it can't be helped. Well, it probably *could* have…'

'Just get on with it, Bethany!'

Bethany looked at him for a few seconds. She wanted

to imprint this image of him in her head. It wasn't a great image because he was as angry as hell with her, although not quite as angry as when he had first arrived. However, it would prove to be a far more comforting image of him than the one which would be presented after she had fully explained herself.

'I told my parents that you were involved in building all sorts of stuff in…well…in dangerous places…places where there are no amenities…for example in the depth of Africa and in war-torn zones…you know, doing your bit to help ease the suffering of helpless victims all over the world…'

Cristiano shook his head as though that simple gesture would sort out her confusing babble. Then he ran his fingers through his hair before staring at her with a perplexed frown.

'I *build all sorts of stuff in dangerous places*? What sort of stuff?'

'I don't know! Stuff. Schools! Community centres! Medical facilities!'

'In the *depths of Africa*?'

'Some of them, yes. And other areas where there's conflict, so to speak.'

'I don't get it. Have you lost your mind? I realise that you must be a compulsive liar, but what the hell did you think you were playing at?'

'You weren't supposed to find out!'

'I must be missing something here, but what exactly was the *point* of turning me into some kind of do-gooder? No, let me ask you something even more fundamental. What was the point of telling your parents about me in the first place? It wasn't as though they were ever going to find out and, even if they had, it's the twenty-first century. However moralistic your parents are, surely they're up to speed with the fact that men and women have relationships, some of which don't last for ever! You have two sisters! Are you going to tell me that both of them have spent a lifetime saving themselves for the right guy and have never been on a date with a man in the meanwhile?'

'No, of course not!'

'Then why the elaborate confession to two people who could happily have remained in the dark? And why not just stick to the facts? You met a guy. You had fun for a couple of weeks. The end.' A brief silence greeted this clearly rational observation, during which Bethany's colour went from shell-pink to scarlet as she prayed for the ground to open and swallow her up or, even more unlikely, for her to open her eyes, blink twice, stretch and realise that the past few months had been nothing more than a weirdly convoluted dream.

'Is your obsession with lying so rampantly out of control?' Cristiano looked at her with narrowed eyes as he tried to get his head round her bizarre admission. 'If so, then you need to seek help.' He stood up. 'And I refuse to go along with this deception.'

Bethany scrambled to her feet and grabbed his hand. The physical contact sent a sharp burst of red-hot awareness rushing through her at speed and she immediately dropped her hand.

'Wait! I'm not finished!'

'No?' Cristiano's mouth curled into a derisive smile. 'More to come? Aside from the missionary service to parts of the world I've never so much as visited? I'm struggling to think of what more you can add to my glowing recommendations.'

'Can we sit back down? Please? I realise you probably think that you've entered a mad house…but there are some other things you…you need to know…'

Only because she looks particularly fetching with that desperate, wide-eyed look on her face...and, hell, the woman was born to be a roller coaster ride, so where was the harm in giving her another few minutes...?

Bethany was relieved that he had listened to her. Having watched the clock like a hawk before her parents had arrived, she was now watching it again in anticipation of them coming down the stairs and making a straight line for the sitting room, where the conversation would go who knew where. Time suddenly seemed a commodity in very limited supply.

'I said all those things because...what we had was rather more involved as far as my parents are concerned. And before I tell you what I mean by that...' She half wished that he would interrupt with something nasty and accusatory instead of just looking at her in silence waiting for her to carry on. Her hands, still tucked protectively in the long sleeves of her baggy jumper, were clammy.

'Before I tell you what I mean by that...' she repeated, stretching that one harmless sentence out for as long as she possibly could, 'I just want you to know that I sent you to all those places...'

'Central Africa, you mean? War-torn zones?'

Bethany nodded. 'I sent you there because it would have been easy for you to disappear...'

'Easy. For. Me. To. Disappear.'

'I mean I could have sent you to New York or Tokyo or even the other side of the planet...New Zealand, maybe, but it would have made things more complicated...'

Cristiano nearly choked at the notion that things could get more complicated than they already were. Bethany, staring off into the distance, relieved that she was unburdening herself because she had known that it would come to this the second he had walked through the front door, hardly noticed his staggered expression.

'But if you were based in say…*the Congo*…then our relationship could just have drifted. I mean, how easy would it be for an engaged couple to keep up their relationship across such a hefty distance?'

'Engaged couple?'

Bethany, once again looking at him, nodded and slowly extended her hand to reveal a very discreet engagement ring. 'It's not real, of course, but I had to have something to show Mum and Dad.'

He hadn't noticed the ring, but then he hadn't been paying much attention to her hands and he realised now that she had kept them out of sight as much as she could, tucked up in those long sleeves of hers. Cristiano stared at her in utter disbelief.

'You think I'm nuts, don't you?'

'Nuts? That's putting it mildly.'

'Okay. Hear me out. I know you might be a bit angry…' Her keen ears detected the sounds of approaching parents. It was now or never and never wasn't an option. 'I had to tell this little white lie…'

'Little white lie? Please, do me a favour and define *big*!'

'Because, like I said, Mum and Dad are pretty old fashioned and they would have been bitterly disappointed if they had known that their daughter had had a two week fling with a guy abroad and returned home pregnant.'

CHAPTER FIVE

CRISTIANO finally discovered what it felt like to have a bomb detonate in the epicentre of his life. He stared at her in stunned silence and he could feel the colour draining away from his face. He looked, Bethany thought, like a man who had leapt out of a plane only to find that he'd forgotten his parachute. He was in shocked free fall and she could understand why. From being a carefree, single guy he was now an engaged man with a kid on the way. All in the space of a couple of hours and, worse than that, he was engaged to a woman whom he considered a scheming liar with an eye to the main chance. Did it get any worse?

With impeccable timing, her parents arrived on the scene, postponing the inevitable showdown, for which Bethany was grateful, although it might have been better for her to have just got it out of the way. As it was, they were both at the mercy of both her parents, who had innumerable tales to tell of their dearest daughter and her fabulously loving childhood where money was stretched to its limit, what with three children and their menagerie of pets. And then, when her mother had disappeared to rustle up something to eat, at the mercy of her father who immediately installed a drink in Cristiano's hand and called him to account on his many varied travels.

'Africa,' he mused, settling down on the sofa for the long

haul. 'Never been there myself. Must have been a hell of an experience for you. Great to know that there are still young people out there who care enough, though, son.'

Bethany groaned to herself as her father tilted his head to one side and looked at Cristiano with keen interest.

'Cristiano…' She cleared her throat and smiled weakly at her dad. 'He…er…doesn't really like to talk about his good works out in…um…Africa…and other places…He's very modest…you know…' She hazarded a laugh, which fizzled out into silence. Thanks to her parents' happy belief that they were really engaged, she had found herself stuck next to Cristiano on the sofa, which was richly ironic, she felt, considering the only reason he would choose to be this close would be to strangle her. Now, he reached across and gathered her hand in his and gave it a little squeeze.

'That's very sweet of you to say that, Bethany…' He turned to her profile and was gratified to see that she was as jumpy as a cat on a hot tin roof. Doubtless her poor innocent father would put all that blushing and trembling down to her delight at her so called fiancé's unexpected arrival but he knew better. 'But don't you remember all those pictures I showed you…?'

'Pictures?' She turned to look at him and tried, uselessly, to wriggle her hand out of his grasp.

'You know the pictures…the ones in my album, *my Africa album*.'

'Oh, yes, right.'

'So why don't *you* give your dad the gist of what I did over there…?' He gave her hand another squeeze and felt her dig her nails into his palm, at which point he promptly released her fingers, only to insinuate his hand on her thigh, a gesture of demonstrable affection, except to her. His smile of encouragement earned him a thinly concealed glare and it was all he could do not to tell her how much he was going to enjoy watching her dig herself out of her lies.

Bethany read all of that in his fleeting look and that warm smile on his lips was anything *but* encouraging. She took a deep breath and crossed her fingers behind her back as she launched into a flowery description of a community centre which was one hundred per cent lifted from something she had recently seen on television. As she finally came to a stop, she heard Cristiano say softly, 'Now *that* deserves a round of applause.' He looked at John. 'Your daughter has a very persuasive way with words. She could sell snow to the Eskimos…couldn't you, *darling*?'

Bethany braved his eyes, which were coolly at odds with the smiling mouth. She forced herself to smile back. At least in the company of her parents she would have to try to look enraptured or, if not enraptured, at least pleased that her gallivanting fiancé had turned up.

Seen from another angle, she guessed that the farce being enacted might have seemed hysterically funny. Unfortunately, caught in the middle of it, it was more tragedy than comedy.

'I don't know about that,' Bethany muttered, but Cristiano was undeterred.

'I mean—' he turned to face her father but his hand remained firmly glued to her thigh, a gentle reminder that he was right here on the sofa next to her and was not going to let her out of his reach until he was good and ready '—when she described her house here, in Ireland, I almost got the impression that she was talking about a castle!'

'Couldn't be further from the truth, as you can see!' John shook his head, smiling at his daughter. 'But you're right. I know she's going to pull a face when I say this, but our Bethany was always top of the class in her English!'

'I can well imagine.'

'But now that circumsta…'

From the kitchen, Bethany heard her mother carolling them in for dinner and she breathed a small sigh of relief. Her father preceded them and it gave her a vital chance to move out of Cristiano's reach as they both stood up.

'Stop it!' she hissed at him under her breath.

'Stop…what?'

'Stop touching me!'

'Now why would you say that?' Cristiano's voice was as hard as nails. 'You're a conscienceless liar and I'm supposed to play the part of the lucky husband-to-be. Surely a bit of touching is only to be expected? And, correct me if I'm wrong, but nothing's been mentioned of any so-called *pregnancy*. Funny, that, wouldn't you say?'

'What are you getting at?'

She was spared an answer to her question by her parents beaming at them as they entered the kitchen. Hand in hand. The loving and now united couple. Bethany reminded herself never to trust appearances. She felt pretty sure that the man standing next to her was thinking the very same thing.

'Just fetched some chicken casserole I had in the freezer,' Eileen confided as they all settled at the long pine table in the kitchen, the surface of which bore the hallmarks of homework past. 'Tell me what you think, Cristiano…' She looked at him expectantly and puffed up with delight when he went into profuse compliment mode while next to him Bethany tortured herself by wondering what he had meant when he had said that it was *funny that her parents hadn't mentioned a word about the pregnancy.* Had he thought that she'd been lying? Made the whole thing up? What if he let slip some killer remark about *never wanting kids?* She racked her brain to remember if he'd ever mentioned anything of the sort. Never had she felt more need for something alcoholic, if only to survive her mother's questions about *where they had met, how they had met*. No amount of attempts to drag the conversation onto neutral territory could derail the older woman from her curiosity. Bethany was only thankful that her father was no longer quizzing him on all those wonderful things he had done in darkest Africa.

What had seemed a good idea at the time, a way of saving her parents from the anguish and disappointment of their daughter turning up on their doorstep pregnant and single, had returned to bite her.

Almost worse was the reality that Cristiano was charming the socks off them. He drew on amusing anecdotes like a magician pulling rabbits out of a hat and it was only when they were clearing away the dishes that Bethany found a sudden spark of inspiration and, while she was loading the dishwasher with her mother, she managed to insert in a casual voice, 'Now you understand what I meant when I told you that he was dashing!'

'Oh, darling. I'm so happy for you. Of course, it's such a shame that you've had to put your university course on hold, but he seems such a lovely guy. I don't think he'd mind one bit if you resumed your studies in due course, do you?'

Bethany leaned against the kitchen counter, ears alert for the sound of any approaching feet from the dashing man in question, who had been taken to the sitting room with her father. 'Well, I might have to…'

'What do you mean?' Eileen paused to look at her daughter with concern.

'I mean…' The sound of yet another lie, piling up on top of the multitude she had already told, raced towards her like a galloping horse that was out of control and Bethany sighed. 'Nothing. I just meant that…it's always good to have a degree up your sleeve.'

'But don't forget that you have other duties now, darling.'

Bethany grimaced. 'Fat chance of me forgetting that.' In truth she had gradually become accustomed to the thought of having a baby. What had been an enormous shock to start with had levelled off to a calm acceptance that her pregnancy wasn't going to go away and she would have to deal with it. It was a blessing that she had had her parents to support her, for continuing with university had been out of the question and she had had no desire to remain in London as a single mother.

'I told your dad not to mention anything about the baby,' Eileen rattled on, as happy as a bunny in a field of carrots. 'I thought you might like to break it to Cristiano yourself and I wasn't sure if you had said anything…'

'Thanks, Mum.'

'You don't seem as thrilled at Cristiano's arrival as I might have expected, Beth,' her mother said anxiously. 'I know you thought that he might be stuck out there for months on end with his building project…'

'But here I am!'

From behind them, and latching on to that last pensive observation, came the all too familiar voice of Cristiano. He strolled across to Bethany and casually slung his arm over her shoulder, pulling her towards him. Reluctantly, Bethany extended her hand around his waist. Through his shirt, she could feel the rock hardness of his body and a convulsive shiver made her feel temporarily giddy.

'And, as I mentioned to John in the sitting room, the bearer of glad tidings, my darling.'

'What's that?' Bethany looked up at him, horribly aware that both her parents were watching them with eagle eyes.

She could almost *hear* her mother's breathless, expectant silence.

'No more projects...'

Bethany's jumble of thoughts lagged behind her mother's and it was only when her mother clapped her hands that it dawned on her exactly what he was saying.

'Yippee!' She tried to insert some enthusiasm into her voice as she watched the last glimmers of any excuse for his disappearance from her life take wing and fly through the window.

'That's right,' Cristiano expanded, just so that she was in no doubt as to what he was saying. 'My priorities are here now. Aren't they, sweetheart? Right here with you and...our baby.'

Suddenly the world was full of rainbows and angels. At least, as far as her parents were concerned. Her mother could barely contain her excitement and while the babble of voices resounded around her Bethany felt nothing but a dull awareness of a situation that was now no longer in her control. Had she thought that she might persuade him to disappear out of her life? He didn't love her. He never had. Yet he had found himself landed with the prospect of fatherhood in a little under four months, welded against his will to a woman he now loathed, a woman he considered an inveterate liar and heaven only knew what else. When had it ever been her dream to find herself expecting a baby by a man she loved who felt nothing but scorn towards her? Since when was that *any woman's* dream?

'I wasn't sure if Beth had mentioned it to you...'

'We were shocked when she broke the news to us...'

'But now that we've met you, we couldn't hope for a better son-in-law...'

'Dad!'

'Of course, we wouldn't dream of rushing you into

anything,' Eileen hastened to add. 'You just have to excuse us because we're a little old-fashioned when it comes to things like that...'

'So, as it happens, is my own mother.' Had he really thought that she had been lying about the pregnancy? She had lied about pretty much everything else but, in that one area, she had been telling the truth. Her father had tactfully asked him whether he knew or whether he had already disappeared to Africa by the time Bethany had found out, and at that split moment in time Cristiano had kissed sweet goodbye to his freedom. Two weeks of fun in the sun and he would be paying the price for the rest of his life. What choice did he have? It was a mess but it was a mess from which he could not walk away. He tried to imagine how his mother and his grandfather would react and for a fleeting few seconds he could understand why she had fabricated this particular lie. His mother would have been devastated if he had shown up with a child in tow and no mother in sight.

'You'll have to tell us all about her...about your family... I'm afraid Bethany has been a bit economical on information...'

Your daughter, it was on the tip of his tongue to tell them, has been economical on a number of things.

'But right now—' John put his arm around his wife with affection '—Eileen and I are going to hit the sack.'

'And we may be old-fashioned—' Eileen gave Cristiano a warm smile '—but we're not so old-fashioned that we expect you two love birds to sleep in different rooms...'

'But *Mum*!' Bethany's voice bordered on a screech. 'You've *never* let Shania or Melanie bring their boyfriends home and share a bedroom!'

'Slightly different situation here, don't you think, pet?'

'Well, yes,' Bethany huffed, 'but that's no reason…I mean, I wouldn't want to disrespect…'

'Thank goodness we got rid of that single bed of yours a few years ago! Remember how upset you were at losing the headboard?' This to Cristiano. 'She had collected a range of stickers on it from when she was just knee high to a grasshopper! Can you believe it? Detached all of them and stuck them in a scrapbook!'

Bethany felt herself go crimson. Did her mother imagine that that somehow made her sound *sweet*? Couldn't she see that the flip side of *sweet* was *fruit loop*, which was what Cristiano was already thinking? No, she thought unhappily, why on earth should her mother think that her dearly beloved and only recently engaged daughter might not want to share a bedroom with her sexy, *dashing, adventurous* fiancé who couldn't wait to rip her to shreds?

With that parting shot her parents, still chatting and laughing with each other, headed off, leaving a brutal silence behind them.

'So…' Cristiano moved so that he was standing in front of her '…where to begin…'

'We can begin with the fact that *I won't be sharing my bedroom with you*. You can have Shania's room. Mum and Dad will never know if I get up early enough and smooth down the quilt.'

'I can think of a better place to start.' He walked towards the kitchen door and shut it. Then, making sure that she couldn't bolt, he remained standing in front of the closed door, six foot two of lethal determination. 'For instance, did you get pregnant on purpose?'

Bethany was horrified at the outrageous insult. She clenched her hands into tight fists and glared at him.

'That's the most idiotic thing I've ever heard!'

'Then you've led a very sheltered life,' Cristiano said

cuttingly. 'From where I'm standing, I'm seeing someone who connived her way into my life…'

'*Connived my way? You* were the one who showed up on my doorstep, don't you remember?'

'Hardly *your* doorstep.'

'Okay, the doorstep!' She pushed her hair away from her face.

'…And, having found my bed, decided that I was just too good a catch to let go and what better way to hold a man than to get pregnant by him?'

Bethany laughed incredulously. 'You think I *planned this*? You really think that I *wanted* to abandon my degree, abandon my independence so that I could have a baby?' Her eyes filled up, her mouth wobbled; she felt like someone on the edge of a nervous breakdown. She was hardly showing her pregnancy but for the past few months it had been on her mind every waking minute. She had been living on a day to day basis, not daring to think beyond the very near future. The dream of finding her feet away from the little town in which she had grown up was in ruins around her and she couldn't face the thought of sitting down and really working out what happened next. It was as though Plan A, around which she had based her future, had devolved into some other plan and she no longer had the right tools to grapple with it. Where would she be in six months' time? A year? Where would she be living? She couldn't very well remain an indefinite lodger in her parents' house with a young baby, still sleeping in the bedroom she had slept in as a child herself. But where would she go? And how would she be able to earn a sufficiently good living to support two?

That he could stand there and coolly ask whether she had planned the pregnancy was just too much!

'Do you really imagine that you're that much of a dream

catch?' She propelled herself angrily away from the counter against which she had been leaning. 'You're *arrogant*, you're *cruel* and you're a massive *snob*!' She poked one shaking finger at him. 'Do you honestly think that I would throw away my future so that I could hitch my wagon to a guy who hates my guts and thinks I'm a cheap liar?' She dashed an angry tear away from her face. 'How sad and... and *desperate* do you think I am?'

'Calm down. You're beginning to get hysterical.' *Arrogant? Cruel? A snob?* Shouldn't *she* be the one on the back foot? To the best of his memory, *he* had been totally upfront with her, so how was it that she was now hurling accusations at *him*?

'It's impossible talking to you.' Bethany was further enraged by the fact that Cristiano was as cool as a cucumber. She felt that if she didn't leave she would explode and the explosion would wake her parents, if not the entire town.

'You're not talking. You're being hysterical.'

'You make me *feel* hysterical!' Her green eyes clashed with his and she felt dizzy and off balance. How was it possible for him to do this to her? To shake her to the very core and make her feel giddy when all she wanted to feel was repulsion?

'You don't *look* pregnant.'

'What?'

'Shouldn't you be bigger?'

Bethany was thoroughly disconcerted by this abrupt change of topic. 'Some people don't show until quite late on and I'm one of those. Why are you changing the subject?'

'Because you shouldn't be getting so overwrought in your...condition.'

'How do you expect me to feel when you stand there like a block of ice sneering at me and accusing me of plotting all of this?' Deep breaths, she thought. Hysteria was no way to deal with the situation. 'If I had been lunatic enough to get pregnant to trap you, then don't you think that I might just have contacted you the minute I found out?'

'Why didn't you?'

'For the same reason that…I took off. I wasn't the rich, worldly-wise woman you thought I was. I was a nobody, the sort of person you wouldn't have looked at twice in the normal course of things.'

'Don't run yourself down,' Cristiano censured, frowning.

'I'm not running myself down, Cristiano. I'm telling it like it is. You told me yourself that you would never date any woman who didn't come from a similar background to you because you would never be sure that she wasn't after you for your money.'

'I never said that!' The conversation seemed to have run away from him and he couldn't figure out where or when he had relinquished control.

'Yes, you did!'

'Okay. Maybe I did, although I'm not convinced.'

'So when I discovered that I was pregnant, I knew that I couldn't contact you. How would you have felt if I'd shown up on your doorstep, one Bethany Macguire, pregnant and average, with nowhere to go and barely a dime to her name? Don't tell me that you would have fallen over yourself with joy and rapture!'

'That's hardly the point.'

'Then what is?'

'I deserved to know. When it comes to a child, it's not about how I would feel or how you would feel, it's about the child. Had you any intention at all of ever contacting me to tell me that I had fathered a child?'

Bethany looked away, reddening. Put like that, she

sounded like a selfish cow, but at the time the thought of telephoning him, explaining herself, explaining that she was going to have a baby, had left her mind almost as quickly as it had entered it.

'I would have. In due course. Most probably.'

Cristiano stamped on his immediate response to that. There was little point in pursuing that line of attack, but in his mind he envisaged a scenario in which his child grew up without him around, became the stepson or stepdaughter of some other man who would have entered her life at some point in time. The thought outraged him. Just thinking of her in the arms of someone else outraged him. He put that thought out of his head and resolved to approach the situation from a practical direction.

He also found himself reluctantly believing her reasons for lying to him in the first place. Which, naturally, didn't excuse her opportunistic manipulation of the truth, but he would overlook that because there were now far bigger things in the mix and that was a reality he couldn't afford to forget.

'I'm surprised you didn't kill me off,' he mused and Bethany looked up at him, again sidetracked by his change of tone. From icy-cold and enraged, his voice was now low and husky and mildly amused. It made the hairs on the back of her neck stand on end and something inside her uncurled, making her feel vulnerable and exposed.

'I'm not *that* horrible,' she stuttered breathlessly. 'Besides, it's just as well that I didn't, considering you've appeared here. Explaining the sudden appearance of an absent fiancé is enough of a nightmare. Explaining one who had come back to life would have been impossible.' With some of her anger defused, she was belatedly aware of just how close she was to him. Practically touching and it was beginning to get to her. She took a couple of steps back and told him that she was going to bed.

'Where are your clothes, anyway?' she asked. Her parents wouldn't have noticed his lack of a suitcase and she only had now.

'A certain large hotel a few miles away, as it happens.'

'Oh, right. The converted manor.' She would have suggested that he drive right back there but what was the point? Her parents would think it bizarre for the newly reunited couple to spend their first night apart, especially when they had shown such remarkable twenty-first century liberalism in allowing them to share the same bedroom. 'So you have no clothes with you. Well, what are you going to sleep in, just out of interest.'

'Tut, tut. Don't tell me that your memory's *that* short.'

A stirring, heady drumbeat started deep inside her, bringing hectic colour to her cheeks as she remembered their nights together. No clothes. For her, that had been a novelty. She had *never* slept in the nude before and the first time she had done so she had been incredibly shy because it was almost more intimate than making love. But Cristiano, on the other hand, didn't even possess a pair of pyjamas.

'No way. And, furthermore, could you please move. I want to go upstairs now.'

Cristiano didn't hesitate to step aside. He wasn't quite sure what the conclusion of their conversation had been. Whether she was Bethany Maguire or Amelia Doni or the Queen of England, she was still as feisty, argumentative and unpredictable as he had remembered and, as usual, he was left feeling as though he had been stuffed in a washing machine and spun at full speed.

Besides, he was interested to see what was going to happen when they made it to her bedroom. He watched her small, rounded derrière with appreciative eyes as she walked ahead of him. One thing he had not forgotten was her delicacy. She was like spun glass and she moved with the grace of a dancer, even though she most likely had never been to a ballet class in her entire life. It was difficult to judge whether she had any kind of bump at all underneath the baggy jumper, but from behind her shape had certainly stayed the same.

For the first time, Cristiano considered the baby she was carrying as opposed to the pregnancy with which he had been presented and decided that it was a great credit to his talent for flexibility and his strength of character that he hadn't immediately felt bitter or trapped. His mother and his grandfather would be over the moon, of that he was sure. It might not have happened in the perfect way, as they would have ideally liked, but the end result would be welcomed with open arms.

They had reached the top of the stairs and Bethany turned to him and pointed down the corridor.

'My bedroom's the last on the right,' she said in a hushed voice. 'I'll be in in a minute and you'd better make sure that you've made yourself a bed on the floor. I'll bring you a spare quilt and you can use one of my pillows.'

Cristiano didn't say anything. He headed for her bedroom, taking his time to have a look at the other rooms he walked past, which were undoubtedly her sisters' rooms, and he was even able to tell which room belonged to which sister. The one with the shelves and shelves of books would be Shania's, and the one with pots of make-up and creams would be Melanie's. Something else, he half mused, that she had not lied about. Her own room was, at the end of the corridor, the biggest, with sprawling windows on two walls and decorated in neutral shades of creams and oatmeal. The furniture was old and heavy and not at all to his taste, but it seemed to suit the feel of the room and the bed was big. Four fluffy pillows, none of which would be going anywhere near the floor, if only she knew.

Cristiano kicked off his shoes, got rid of his socks and then settled down on the feather mattress with satisfaction, his hands clasped behind his head, his mind pleasantly involved in imagining her reaction when she returned with her spare quilt to find him lying on her bed.

He didn't have very long to wait. Literally five minutes later she tiptoed into the room, pausing by the door to get her bearings because he hadn't bothered to switch on the light. It was something she remedied straight away, banging on the switch and then pulsating as she looked at him sprawled out on her bed. She wanted to slam the door hard but resisted the impulse and closed it with a decisive click.

'What are you doing?' She flung the quilt at him and he fielded it expertly onto the floor.

'I'm enjoying the luxury of this great feather mattress of yours. Much more comfortable than the one at the hotel, which shows that money doesn't always buy the best.'

'Well, now that you've enjoyed it, you can get up and start doing something about your sleeping arrangements.' The intimacy of their surroundings was choking her and she had to force her legs into action. 'And these are some of Dad's pyjamas. Put them on.'

'Why? You've already seen me naked.'

'That was then and this is now!'

'Something about horses and stable doors springs to mind here.'

'I don't *care* what springs to mind!' Bethany almost wept with frustration. 'Just go and…and get into the pyjamas…' She breathed deeply. 'The bathroom's next door…'

'Sure.' Cristiano stood up and stretched. 'But I'm not sleeping on the floor.'

'Then *I will*!'

'Oh, no, you won't.' He wasn't smiling as he walked slowly towards her. 'You're going to get into that bed and so am I. I won't have you sleeping on the floor, pregnant.'

'Then *you* sleep on the floor.' Her eyes locked with his and her breathing became shallow and laboured.

'Neither of us is going to be sleeping on the floor and if I come back in here to find that you've done something with that quilt other than stuff it away in the wardrobe then I'm not going to be happy.'

'Oh, and *your* happiness is paramount, naturally!'

He shot her a lazy smile and wondered if he'd actually forgotten how fetching she looked when her eyes were blazing and her colour was up. 'So we agree on something. It's a start.'

Bethany spent three seconds fuming as he unhurriedly left the room, grabbing the towel she had brought in with her and stuck on a chair by the door in passing. Then she moved as though propelled by a rocket. Having already washed her face and brushed her teeth, she flung on her old pyjamas, tartan plaid flannelette that any granny would have been proud of, and got into the bed, making sure to draw the covers up to her chin and position one of the pillows as a barrier between them. She then turned her back to the door and squeezed her eyes tightly shut. Neither protected her from the way her skin tingled as she heard the bedroom door quietly open and shut ten minutes later. He moved so silently that she was only aware of him getting into the bed when it was depressed, almost causing her rigid body to topple over the side.

'I know you're not asleep,' Cristiano said conversationally, 'and, whilst I appreciate that you finally accepted the fact that neither of us was going to sleep on the floor like teenagers at a rock festival, I still don't like the pillow between us, so…' he took the pillow and chucked it on the floor '…that's much better. And now we need to talk.' He rolled over onto his side and Bethany stifled a squeak as she felt the brush of bare skin against her. She was over on her side in a shot and facing him, although she could hardly make out his face.

'Where are Dad's pyjamas?'

'On the floor. I'm in my boxers, though, so there's no need to get your reinforced knickers in a twist.'

The silence settled between them and, with each passing second, Bethany could feel her nerves straining harder.

'You do realise that we need to have a proper conversation, don't you?' Cristiano said calmly. 'By which I mean a conversation without the hysterics.' Fully aware of the full impact barrier she had erected between them by way of her pyjamas and determined not to be distracted, Cristiano was nevertheless aware that his body was riding roughshod over his intentions.

'This isn't a good place to have a conversation.'

'No…? I thought that's where all couples talked. In bed.'

'We're not a couple.'

'Then define what we are, not forgetting that we're engaged.'

Now that her eyes had fully adjusted to the lack of light in the bedroom, Bethany could see him more clearly and she could feel her whole body aching from the torture of being within inches of him. Her double bed might be big for one but it was reduced to the size of a handkerchief with Cristiano taking up more than half of it.

'I wish you wouldn't keep reminding me of that,' she whispered.

'Fine. Then I'll change the topic. After all, I wouldn't want to damage that fragile conscience of yours…so how do you feel about me asking you this…? How has your body changed?'

'I beg your pardon?'

'Your body,' Cristiano murmured huskily. 'How's it changed? I want to feel your stomach. I want to feel my baby.' He reached out and slipped his hand underneath the unflattering checked long-sleeved top which was way too hot to wear to bed. 'I think you'll agree that I have a right…'

CHAPTER SIX

'WHAT are you doing?' Bethany emitted a little squeak of protest and tried to wriggle away from those long fingers but there was limited room to manoeuvre so she had to content herself with a pointless tussle with his hand.

'You hide it well,' Cristiano conceded as he felt the smooth, rounded swell of her stomach. He couldn't believe that he hadn't noticed before she had told him but, then again, he hadn't been looking.

'Don't…' Bethany drew in a shaky lungful of air, her body red-hot and aching as he continued to rub her stomach with the flat of his hand.

'Don't? But I have every right, wouldn't you agree? I am, after all, the prodigal daddy-to-be, just returned from his dangerous stint in the depths of Africa.'

'That's not funny.'

'No, you're right. It's not. Twenty-four hours ago, I was a man with no responsibility to anyone but himself…' He removed his hand from her rounded belly, assailed by the magnitude of the situation.

'Twenty-four hours ago you were a man who was speeding up here to lay into me for deceiving you!'

'Little did I know the depth of the deceit.'

'But you would never have sought me out if you hadn't found out, would you, Cristiano?' Was she hoping that he would contradict her? Her cheeks flamed angrily at the realisation that, yes, fool that she was, she *still* wanted to hear *something* that might indicate that she had been more than just a two week interlude in his busy schedule.

'Did you expect me to?'

'Of course not! So can you blame me for coming back here when I found out that I was pregnant? Can you blame me for not getting in touch with you to tell you the good news?'

'I have no intention of being your accomplice in justifying yourself.'

'You are so...*so superior*!' She balled her hands into fists and gritted her teeth together to stop herself from shouting and bringing her parents flying into the bedroom.

'If by that you mean that I'm upfront with people, then yes, I am.'

'Haven't you ever done something you shouldn't have, Cristiano?'

'Yes, I spent two weeks in Barbados with a woman I barely knew. In retrospect, you might say that that was one of my more spectacular mistakes.'

'That's a horrible thing to say!'

And Cristiano knew it. He also knew that it was a lie but damned if he was going to be the sort of loser who would ever confess that those stolen two weeks had been two of the best he could remember in a long time. Damned if he would give oxygen to that niggling voice in his head that was telling him that yes, he might very well have tried to contact her, *whatever the circumstances of her flight*. What sort of sad man would pursue a woman who had walked out on him? He absolutely refused to admit himself into that category.

'I apologise. Unreservedly.'

'Oh, well, that's all right then.' Bethany gave a strangled

laugh under her breath. She lay on her back and stared up at the ceiling, acutely aware of his steady breathing and the fact that his arm was only a couple of inches away from hers.

In the thick, dark silence Cristiano grudgingly smiled at her sniping response. Okay, so his life had been turned on its head. So had hers. Any other woman, faced with an enraged ex-lover, a man who had the wealth and power to move mountains, a man who had been tricked and conned, would have at least had the decency to be suitably humble. None of that with Bethany. Typically, she was fighting fire with fire and no amount of fighting was going to do any good.

'So now that I have shown up on the scene, none the worse for malaria, famine or curare-tipped arrows, what do you intend to do with me?'

As he expected, a stunning silence greeted that question and he allowed that silence to stretch between them until he could *smell* her tension rising in waves.

'Fortunately, I am prepared to do the decent thing.'

Bethany swung round to look at him in surprise. 'Do the decent thing? What are you talking about?'

'You are pregnant with my baby and I am a man of honour, a man who takes his responsibilities seriously. Naturally, I have no other option but to marry you.'

'Marry me? Have you completely lost your mind?' Bethany gave a snort of laughter. Did he really expect her to leap at his generous offer because he was *a man of honour*, who *took his responsibilities seriously* and, boxed in as he now found himself, would therefore rise to the occasion by *putting a ring on her finger because there was no option*?

'What are you saying?' With one hand, Cristiano reached to the side of the bed and flipped on the light.

Immediately the tiny area around them was thrown into relief. He hoisted himself up on one elbow and looked down at her with a cold frown of incomprehension.

'I'm *saying*...' Bethany sat upright because it felt too weird conducting this conversation when she was horizontal '...that I'm not going to marry you! This isn't the nineteenth century, Cristiano!'

'Well, it's not far off, considering you felt obliged to fabricate an imaginary fiancé for your parents so that you could return here, pregnant!' He was finding it hard to credit that she had just thrown his proposal back in his face! As far as he was concerned, he was one in a million!

'Fabricating an imaginary fiancé is a far cry from walking down the aisle with a man who doesn't even like me!'

'It is pointless bringing emotions into this.'

'What do you mean, *pointless*?'

'Keep your voice down or your parents will be running in here to see what the hell is going on!'

Bethany counted to ten, very slowly. 'Okay. I'm going to keep my voice down because I don't want to create a scene and have Mum and Dad worrying, but I'm not going to marry you, Cristiano. Not in a million years. It might have been stupid for us...not to have been as careful as we should have been, but it would be even more stupid for us to sacrifice our lives for the sake of this baby.'

Eyes blazing, Cristiano flung himself out of the bed and walked across to the window, a vision of semi-naked masculine beauty which drew Bethany's eyes like a magnet.

'I have no idea why you're so taken aback,' she informed his erect back. 'Most women would have leapt at your offer and where would that have left you? Trapped in a marriage which would become a cage for you...for both of us...' He was a man with a strong libido and it didn't take a genius to work out that two and two would inevitably lead to four. He had no feelings for her and it wouldn't be long before he would stray. She would be no more than the mother of his child, to whom fidelity would hold no outstanding advantages.

'So what,' Cristiano said in a soft voice, 'do you suggest?' He felt it was important to maintain a practical note to the conversation but it was taking every ounce of self discipline not to give way to his temper. Virtually as soon as he had known of the situation, he had been aware of what had to be done and he was shocked that his offer of marriage had met with a negative response. She obviously wasn't thinking straight and, whilst he might have been inclined to put that down to hormones, which apparently affected some women during pregnancy, he was forced to conclude that her mind did not work in the same way as his. Nor, for that matter, did it work in the same way as most of the human race, or at least most of the female contingent. She had been spot on when she had remarked that most women would have leapt at his offer.

Bethany couldn't help it. She felt a thread of disappointment snake through her at his ready acceptance of an alternative plan. Had he only proposed marriage as a way of clearing his conscience? Decent guy, duty done, offer rejected so time to move on. She could practically hear his sigh of relief whipping through the air between them.

'Well, you'll have to stay a day or two, I guess. Or it might look a bit odd…'

Cristiano folded his arms and inclined his head to one side. It was in his nature to contradict the stupidity of what she was saying but he was also sharp enough to know that jumping in with his opinions would only provoke yet another bout of high drama and her immediate stubborn retreat.

Bethany licked her lips and looked to him for some verbal encouragement. Finding none, she continued slowly, 'Then you'd have to return to London…you know, because you can't very well stay here for ever… My parents know that you're a businessman, first and foremost…'

'And where do you fit in to this neat little picture?'

'I'd stay here, of course.'

'Why of course? Wouldn't your parents think it a bit strange that you remain behind?' There were more holes in her story than a colander and he had to fight down the sarcasm which threatened to spill out.

'I could always tell them that it would just be more…re-assuring for me to have them around, seeing that your business takes you all over the world. At a moment's notice.'

'I thought I'd already made it clear that there were no more *projects*?'

'Well, you *do* travel, don't you?' Bethany said irritably. 'Why can't you help me out here? Can't you see that I'm just trying to do what's right for both of us?'

'I think it's time we both got some sleep.'

He began walking back towards the bed and she followed his movements with restless, anxious eyes.

'But we haven't sorted out anything.'

'I'm tired. I'm going to sleep. Feel free to let that fertile little imagination of yours run riot with suggestions as to what the next step should be.' He got into the bed, turned on his side with his back to her and ignored her frantic scrabbling movements as she tried to wrest some of the quilt for herself.

Five minutes later and Bethany could hear the soft breathing of a man who had succumbed to sleep. It took her an hour before she felt her own eyelids begin to droop, during which time she had developed serious stiffness in her arms and legs from trying to remain as still as she possibly could.

The next time she opened her eyes, it was to find herself face to face with Cristiano, their noses practically touching. In the course of sleep, they had somehow become entwined. Her leg had managed to insert itself between his thighs and his arm was flung round her.

His eyes were closed and his face was all hard angles barely visible in the darkness. Like a thief, she stole the opportunity to look at him. He couldn't see her. She could linger on his face, allow herself to express her feelings with her guard down.

She wanted to reach out and trace the contours of his mouth and eyes and nose. She used to do that when they were lovers. He had found it amusing, the way she would stare at him as though he was the most riveting man on the face of the earth. She had never, ever seen anyone as beautiful as him.

She was going through a mental checklist of all the things she found so attractive about the way he was put together when he opened his eyes. Fast asleep one minute. Wide-eyed and alert the next. Bethany gave a little gasp and tried to pull away but he snuggled up against her, drawing her against his body.

'You're awake!' she whispered accusingly and Cristiano grinned.

He laced his fingers through her tumbled hair and brought her closer against him. She was no longer making a show of trying to wriggle away, he noticed. He hadn't realised how quiet it was out here in the depths of the countryside. He was accustomed to the constant undercurrent of noise, even in the early hours of the morning. It was so still that he could hear her jerky breathing.

His arousal was fast and hard and he knew the very

instant she became aware of it by her soft whimper. Even though he had only spent a little over a fortnight in her company, it had been an intense experience and he seemed to be able to read her tiniest little reactions. Like the way she had shifted her body fractionally, getting just a tiny bit closer to him. He was surprised to find that he was holding his breath, not wanting to splinter the moment.

'I missed you,' he confessed roughly. 'You left and I couldn't get you out of my head.'

Bethany felt as though a gust of air had whipped her up and carried her off to cloud nine. She sighed and squirmed and closed her eyes and threw her head back with a little moan as his hand circled her stomach, retracing the gentle, tentative exploration he had begun earlier but this time extending it to include her breasts.

'I thought about touching you a thousand times.' Cristiano cupped one of her breasts in his hand, feeling its enlarged weight. 'Your breasts have grown.'

'Yes,' Bethany said in a strangled voice.

'Your nipples will have grown too. Have they? Become larger?'

'Cristiano…' His words made her pulses race. She felt like someone caught in the grip of a fever. No, caught in a raging inferno, one that had been sparked the minute he had walked through the front door.

'Shh…' He leant over her and her mouth parted to receive his questing tongue. His kiss became deeper, more urgent and, as she felt him throb against her, she frantically wanted to rid herself of the crazy toe to neck barrier of her flannelette pyjamas, which she had worn in an attempt to stifle her sexuality.

'I want to see you,' Cristiano told her in a hoarse voice. He didn't give her time to answer. She was soft and compliant and he didn't want to give her the slightest opportunity to gather herself into attack mode. He pushed up the long sleeved top and lost himself in wordless appreciation of her breasts.

He wondered how he could have deluded himself into thinking that his life would slot back to normality the minute he returned to London. *This* had been on his mind for months and he couldn't get enough of her. What was it with this woman? She made him lose control and he abandoned the struggle to resurrect it.

Instead, he grazed his tongue over her pouting nipples, bigger and darker than before. Her body was preparing itself for the birth of their baby and the thought of that was a massive turn-on. His mouth replaced his tongue as he sucked on one nipple, pulling it into his mouth and enjoying the way she was shivering and shuddering underneath him. One hand cupped her breast and the other wandered down, curving over her stomach, which had been practically invisible when she had been decked out in her oversized camouflage gear but was decidedly round and plump when bared. He slipped his hand beneath the elasticated waistband of the pyjamas, moving lower still.

Bombarded by sensation, Bethany arched back and the rasp of his mouth suckling on her nipple became unbearably exquisite. She curled her fingers into his thick, dark hair, steering him towards her other breast. She literally felt as if she couldn't get enough of him. When he raised his head to ask her whether it was safe, whether it was all right, she found herself nodding and telling him *not to stop*.

He made a running commentary on her body, on its changes, and the low velvety words were as erotic as his hands running along her. She was panting as he licked his way along her stomach and then his tongue was in her, flicking and squirming until she was bucking under the ex-

quisite torment. He had teased her like this before, bringing
her to the brink and then waiting for her to subside, but now
there was no lull in his hunger and, before she could pull
back, he had taken her over the edge. Wave upon wave of
pleasure sent convulsive shudders through her body and,
when she finally stilled, he heaved himself over her and
grinned.

'Felt good?'

Bethany said something that emerged as a breathy
whimper, which made him grin some more.

'We shouldn't have done that,' she said weakly.

'Why are you using the past tense?'

There was no way that he was going to let her gather her
thoughts. She had already done way too much thinking as
far as he was concerned. He silenced her with his mouth,
kissing her with lingering thoroughness.

'You're very sexy, pregnant,' he whispered.

'No, I'm not.'

'You are to me.' He parted her thighs with his hand,
taking time to feel the moisture between her legs that was
an indication of how aroused she was. 'We men are simple
creatures,' he murmured, teasing her with his erection,
which had her moving against him so that his hard shaft
rubbed against her sensitised clitoris. 'Evidence of our
virility can't help but prove satisfying. Call it a weird
macho thing.' Never before had he felt so liberated as he
thrust into her, gently at first, then deeper and harder as
their rhythm picked up speed. From the very first time
they had made love, their bodies had been extraordinarily
attuned and nothing had been lost in the months between
the last time they had been together. They moved as one.
Maybe that was why making love to her had always been
such an amazing experience.

Spent from a climax that ranked right up there as one

of the best experiences of his life, Cristiano rolled onto his back, content that things had been sorted between them.

'That was a mistake.'

Her words, crashing through his good mood, took a few seconds to register, then he turned to her, half thinking that he might not have heard her correctly.

'What are you talking about?'

'We shouldn't have made love. And now I'm going to have a shower and I'm going to freeze to death in the process because the central heating's gone off.' She made as if to slip out of the bed and the restraining hand that reached out to circle her wrist was as quick as a whip, dragging her back to him.

'Not so fast,' Cristiano grated. 'You're not ducking out of this conversation. What the hell do you mean by *we shouldn't have made love*? I didn't hear you complaining five minutes ago.'

'I'm not saying that I'm not attracted to you,' Bethany whispered, not daring to look him in the face. 'But that doesn't mean anything.'

'You have no idea what you're talking about.'

'Don't pretend to know me better than I know myself!' she said fiercely, deeply ashamed at the ease with which she had fallen back into his arms. When a clear head had been needed, she had abandoned hers and leapt right back on to the emotional roller coaster ride, as if she hadn't been battered enough by it.

'But I *do* know you better than you know yourself,' Cristiano purred with lethal assurance. 'I know, for instance, that you haven't got a clue how to handle this situation.'

'How dare you?'

'Because I need to do the thinking for both of us,' he told her calmly. 'And spare me another of your hissy fits.

I've listened to everything you've had to say and now you're going to lie back and listen to the voice of reason and common sense.'

'I don't believe I'm hearing this.'

'Well, start believing it. And I'll keep it simple. You're pregnant and, whether you like it or not, I'm not about to disappear on an extended trip to anywhere. I'm not going to be conveniently vanishing to Afghanistan to set up a medical centre. I won't be revisiting Central Africa to see how that non-existent community centre's doing. Nor will I become the callous ex-lover who thinks nothing of leaving his pregnant fiancée for months on end to cope on her own, giving her a handy excuse for the relationship to fizzle out because who can be expected to stay with a complete bastard? Face up to those facts and then we might be getting somewhere.'

'Okay. So maybe you don't *have* to disappear. I'm willing for you to have some involvement…'

'Oh, now, that's remarkably generous of you,' Cristiano told her with biting sarcasm. 'Do you suggest I travel over here once a month to see how things are coming along?'

'It's not that difficult. The air and road links are very efficient.'

'Not efficient enough. I live in London and London is where you will be, like it or loathe it.' He raked his fingers through his hair and sighed in sheer frustration. What was her problem? Why was she so intent on fighting him every inch of the way when he had risen to the occasion in such a superb fashion?

'Do you think you can win me over by trying to force my hand, Cristiano?'

'*Trying to force your hand?* I offered you marriage and you turned me down, even though it is the only reasonable solution and a pretty good one from where I'm standing. It isn't as though we aren't attracted to one another. We are. You can say what you want about it being a mistake that we made love but we were only doing what two people do when they want one another.'

'And, as far as you're concerned, good sex and a sense of duty is enough for a marriage?' She dispelled the lump in her throat and snapped her hand out of his grip. 'So if you had, say, accidentally got another woman pregnant, would your solution have been the same? A marriage of convenience for the sake of the baby?'

'That's a hypothetical question and I'm not into answering hypothetical questions.' But it lodged somewhere in his brain and, although he was not accustomed to ever going down the road of self-indulgent, pointless introspection, he was a little shaken to realise he harboured doubts about whether in similar circumstances he would have committed to marriage with any of the women he had dated in the past, however fine their credentials had been. Maybe it was because none of them had ever been so challenging, maybe it was because this relationship had not had time to run its natural course. He decided that nothing was to be gained from thinking about it. They were in a unique situation, end of story. 'You attack me for asking you to marry me. Have you stopped to think that the child would benefit from having both parents? I come from an extremely conventional family. I had the benefit of both a mother and a father on the scene. I find it inconceivable for you to blithely assume that the absence of one parent is a good thing.'

'I never said that it was a *good thing*. You're putting words into my mouth...'

'I'm putting sensible ideas into your head...'

Bethany found herself thinking about what it might have been like to have grown up without her dad and she resented the fact that he was trying to imply that she was selfish. Selfish for wanting a life that didn't involve her being married to a man who neither liked nor respected her, a man who saw her as an obligation that had to be taken on. He casually accepted that the sex was good, and maybe he saw that as a kind of temporary bonus, and maybe, if she wasn't in love with him, she could have gone along with the proposition. But she *did* love him and to trade herself in as a suitable business deal so that his traditionalism could be satisfied would be like opening a wound and pouring salt in.

'It's not sensible to sign away your life for the sake of convention. Two unhappy people don't add up to a healthy environment for a child. Yes, two parents on the scene is ideal, but two *happy* parents.'

'We were both pretty happy ten minutes ago,' Cristiano pointed out, 'and I'm pretty sure that, given half a chance, we could both be pretty happy again.'

'No, we could *have sex* again! Which isn't going to happen, by the way. It was a moment of madness and...'

'...we had many of those when we were in Barbados, if I recall. All things come with a price.'

'And I'm willing for us to be...friends...' Lying in bed with him, telling him that she was willing to be *friends*, after they had made love, almost brought on a fit of hysterical laughter. 'I'm willing for you to have...whatever input you need to satisfy your conscience...'

Cristiano gritted his teeth but didn't say a word. Her emotional, highly feminine thinking did nothing for him. They had been presented with a problem. He had the solution to it and he didn't see why she couldn't accept it without digging her heels in and stubbornly putting forward a list of arguments that made no sense. And what was with the *friendship* talk? The fact that she was as physically attracted to him as he was to her made a nonsense of that.

Bethany waited for him to try and demolish her suggestion, but he didn't and she continued hesitantly, 'I mean… we shouldn't deny ourselves a chance of happiness with someone else…' She made a valiant effort to try and imagine someone else with whom she could be happy but she couldn't get past Cristiano's forceful, darkly handsome face.

'What does that mean?'

'There could be a guy out there for me, a guy who wants to marry me for who I am, and not because he's duty bound…!'

Cristiano felt a smouldering aggression overwhelm his ability to think rationally. It was an effort to remain lying on the bed next to her, his eyes fixed on the ceiling, his hands loosely linked behind his head. The thought of her with another man was beyond unacceptable. It was outrageous.

'What sort of guy? Someone from around here?'

'Maybe…' Bethany tried the thought on for size. She still knew quite a few of the guys with whom she had gone to school, guys who had remained in the town or close by. They would run a mile from a woman with another man's baby in tow, which was a depressing enough thought, but even more depressing was the certainty that she would not have looked at any of them in a million years, even if they were to give her a second glance. Why bother with minnows when there was a predatorial shark cruising in the waters? Why bother with being sensible when she knew that it only ran skin-deep?

'It would take a saint to commit to a relationship with a woman who was pregnant with another man's baby.' Cristiano subdued his mounting rage to keep his voice level. 'Especially another man who had no intention of leaving an open field.' Now more than ever, it seemed imperative to nail the marriage suggestion. He was not going to idly sit by and watch someone else usurp his role as father. Jealousy and possessiveness, two emotions which were anathema to him, rose up like bile in his throat but he knew, with the instincts of someone adept at reading situations and people, that trying to impose his forceful personality on her would have her running for cover. She might have rosy ideas of some gormless local lad who would tiptoe round her and pander to her every need but she was mistaken on every single count, the foremost one being that he would simply not allow that situation to happen. He had to restrain himself from pointing out what, to him, was an inescapable truth. She was headstrong, stubborn and explosively unpredictable. She would eat most men up and it was very fortunate for her that he wasn't most men.

But she wasn't going to listen to the voice of reason and that being the case, he would just have to adopt a different voice. Same result but a different approach. He felt smugly proud at the level of tolerance which he was—unusually—exhibiting.

'But…' he shrugged in the darkness and shifted away from her '…I'm willing to go along with the friendship card. Like it or not, we are going to be parents and I will not allow us to be parents at war. Now, I think I'm going to get some sleep.' He settled himself further, felt the brush of her leg against his back and briefly contemplated how admirably swift his turnaround had been. From the bottom of his world dropping out, he had rapidly regrouped and seen the advantages of the institution of marriage in which he had previously harboured next to no interest.

Firstly, it would provide the ideal environment in which his child could be raised, happy and well balanced.

Secondly, it would satisfy every member of his family, not least his mother, who would greet the news with enthusiasm, of that he was one hundred per cent sure.

Thirdly, he would have her. This last seemed vitally important to him and he assumed it was because his hunting instinct had been sharpened by her refusal to have him as her husband. With a long history of women who would do anything for him, he had at last met his match in a woman who, seemingly, would put herself out to do absolutely nothing for him. Except in bed, where she lost all her control. Just thinking about that loss of control threatened to undo his calm frame of mind.

All things considered, Cristiano was feeling pretty good by the time he finally fell asleep.

He awoke to a heavy grey light which could barely manage to filter through the thick curtains, and an empty bed. He had slept like the proverbial log and felt all the better for it. Accustomed to rarely venturing out without his laptop computer, BlackBerry and generally complete access to the outside world, he realised that he was now cut off from civilisation, at least until he got back to the hotel later in the morning and, surprisingly, he was okay with the situation.

He rolled over onto his back and then heaved himself onto his elbows at the sight of Bethany framed in the doorway, fully dressed in a full skirt and another baggy sweater, this time in a different colour. He absent-mindedly wondered how she managed to make such a shapeless outfit look so tempting. He had a vivid and instant recall of the feel of her swollen breasts in his hands and the taste of her nipples on his tongue and his body responded with alacrity.

'I see you're up.' She entered the room and shut the door quietly behind her because, from personal experience, walls in her parents' house tended to have ears.

She had postponed going back into the bedroom until the last possible moment. In fact, until her mother had more or less demanded that she wake Cristiano so that he could partake of the full Irish breakfast which she had made especially.

Cristiano refrained from making the obvious quip about being up in more than one sense. Instead, he informed her that he had not had such a good night's sleep in a long time. Bethany, who felt punch-drunk from her restless night, scowled and was disgruntled when he grinned broadly in return.

'You have no clothes,' she said, eyeing his bronzed torso, which he was making little attempt to conceal. 'What are you going to wear?'

'Oh, I can go back to the hotel and get them.'

'Have you looked outside the window?'

Cristiano obliged, slipping out of bed, glimpsing her rise in colour as he did so. It had snowed and it was a spectacular sight. The fields which fell away from the back of the house were a landscape of pristine, virgin white. The sky was a yellow grey, dull and threatening and still releasing its heavy load. He dropped the curtain and turned to her.

'So...' he spread his arms wide, unperturbed by the uninviting expression on her face '...tell me what you want me to do...You call the shots...'

CHAPTER SEVEN

CRISTIANO found out soon enough. After a hearty breakfast, the like of which he had not tasted since he had been
a teenager with an insatiable appetite and an abundance
of free time that could be apportioned to satisfying it, he
found himself with a checklist of things to do, which he
was pretty sure Bethany had compiled with a great deal
of satisfaction. Most of the chores necessitated him being
outside and, since he had not a stitch of clothing with him,
aside from what he had arrived in, which were in the process of being washed, he was obliged to brace near blizzard
conditions in some of her father's clothes, which were too
short in the arms and legs and too large in the waist.

'Clear drive…and salt…chop wood for logs…milk and
bread from corner shop…' He lounged against the door-
frame and looked up from the list. 'Sure this is all? There
must be a few *more* outdoor duties you need me to fulfil…'
She was busying herself by the kitchen sink, the picture
of domesticity were it not for the smirk on her face. She
sauntered up to him, took the list, read it slowly with a
thoughtful frown and then returned it to him.

'Nope. That's all *for the moment.* Why? Do you think
the Mr Perfect image might come a bit unglued by all the
heavy outdoor work?' It still rankled that his charm offen-
sive had been relentless and highly successful over break-

fast. He had made himself useful in the kitchen, despite her mother's protests that she was fine, and had won her father over with his ridiculous knowledge of Irish politics, horse racing and tips on investments for pension funds, which seemed to be her father's most recent area of concern.

In the process, he had practically ignored her and she had had to remind herself that that was all to the good, considering they were now just *friends*. He had listened to what she had said, had backed off and the situation was now perfect. Fabulous. Of course, she would have to think about her story when it came to letting her parents down with the wedding that would never be, but she would cross that bridge when she came to it. In the meantime, she decided that satisfaction was the order of the day. She had got exactly what she had wanted! His respect! He had understood the situation and would no longer think that he could subject her to his unwanted attentions. She was uncomfortably aware that she had to gloss over that last thought but the end result was the same. He was keeping his distance and if her parents were blissfully unaware of the slight shift in the atmosphere, then *she* was very much aware of it. There had been no more of those suggestive looks or accidental brushing of hands or innuendo.

'My *Mr Perfect* image… Now, should I take that as a compliment, I wonder?'

Bethany had a moment of wishing that her parents were around like chaperones because the lazy gleam in his eyes was mesmerising. She had to pull herself back down to earth and slam the door shut on a mind that wanted to play with the taboo images of running her fingers over his shirt, undoing the buttons, slipping her hand underneath to feel his warm skin.

The outfit which she had chosen for him, having told her parents that he had left his clothes at the hotel into which he had booked *just in case she had not been at home when he had arrived*, should have reduced his sex appeal to zero. It was one of her father's oldest shirts. Something he used to wear for gardening a thousand years ago, a checked flannel number with two buttons missing, frayed cuffs and faded to the point that the original colour was no longer obvious. The very opposite of the handmade Italian shirts Cristiano favoured. The trousers were of a similar age and needed a belt. His handstitched leather shoes had been exchanged for green wellies, and the waterproof anorak she had supplied was heavy and shapeless. She had also insisted, under cover of the caring girlfriend, that he wear a woollen hat to combat the thickly falling snow and deep, penetrating cold.

'Wouldn't want you catching your death out there,' she had said, smiling smugly when she had handed him the bundle of clothes. 'We wrap up warm in this part of the world. No time for silly designer clothes...'

'Understood,' Cristiano had said, leaning in to her so that his warm breath had fanned against her cheek. 'I would know all about the pointlessness of designer clothes, having spent so much time in Central Africa on that project, wouldn't I?'

Bethany looked at him now and folded her arms. 'I know you've probably never done a day's hard work in your entire life—' she began and he cut her short before she had time to finish her sentence.

'And your assumptions would be based on...what, exactly?'

'You're a company man, Cristiano,' she stammered, sticking her chin up. 'You sit behind a desk...'

'Every summer when I was at university I worked on a building site,' he informed her succinctly. He straightened up and pushed himself away from the door. 'I've always thought that work that stretches the body is good for the brain and excellent for maintaining a healthy balance. Even now, I make sure that my trips to the gym are as physically gruelling as possible. So do me a favour and try not to pigeonhole me.' He slung on the borrowed anorak which, Bethany thought sourly, had never looked like that on her father. 'In fact, when I'm done with this list of things, I might just join your father in the fields and help out with the cattle. Now, why don't you be a good little girl and run along and make sure that my clothes are nicely laundered…?'

'How dare you…?'

'What?' Cristiano threw her a mocking smile over his shoulder as he headed out. 'Pigeonhole you?'

She was still smarting from the way he had neatly turned the verbal tables on her when, a couple of hours later, she indeed found herself fishing his clothes out of the tumble dryer and setting up the ironing board so that she could iron his shirt.

'Women don't do this stuff any more,' she complained to her mother, who had taken it as a given that Cristiano's clothes, once washed, would be returned to him in the sort of pristine condition in which they had originally been bought from the shop, or tailor or wherever he stocked up on his mega-expensive outfits.

'If you're tired, I don't mind running the iron over them,' her mother said placidly, taking time out from the stew she was in the middle of making.

'I'm fine,' Bethany muttered in a driven tone. 'I was just saying that the days of toiling over an ironing board, ironing a man's shirt and trousers are over.'

'Oh, I don't think it's asking too much for Cristiano to come back here to some nice, clean, pressed clothing, do you? Not when he's been making himself so helpful around the house when he's probably exhausted and in need of a rest himself after everything he's been through. And your dad said that he's had the best advice off him about what to do with his savings, better than that accountant in Limerick he's been using.'

Bethany's teeth snapped together on the tart retort to her mother's eulogy. She debated letting the sizzling iron sit on the pristine white shirt just long enough for it to leave a hideous indelible stain.

'He's certainly a gem when it comes to finances,' she managed. Shirt and trousers finished, she switched off the iron and stood it upright on the ironing board for it to cool.

'The man seems to be a gem when it comes to most things,' her mother mused with a smile. 'A rare find. I'd be more than pleased if your sisters decided to bring home a couple of those for my prospective sons-in-law.'

In a minute she would start making noises about weddings and honeymoons. Bethany could feel it hovering in the warm, aromatic air between them and she sighed.

'Mum...I've been having some doubts about...you know...marrying Cristiano...' She felt awkward colour seep into her face, intensifying as her mother stopped stirring the pot and looked at her, open-mouthed.

'I really wasn't going to say anything...' It had to be done. The longer the charade continued, the more difficult it would be to back out of an impossible situation and also, what on earth was she going to do when Cristiano returned to London? Go back with him? Live where? In his apartment? Where they would work on their *friendship*, while she fell deeper and harder for the man? Would she have to sit around and watch as he went out with other women? Pretend that none of it mattered? Because the only thing that did was the child they had accidentally created together?

'Sit down, Beth. I'm going to make you a cup of tea. In fact, I think I'll make us both a cup of tea.'

'I've been thinking,' she said, hands round the mug of sweet tea, 'that everything happened really quickly with Cristiano. I know you're going to tell me that it was like that with you and Dad but things are different these days. Marriage isn't the immediate option. I just don't feel I know him well enough to tie the knot...' Her mother's expression was altering from concerned and anxious to disappointed but valiant with it.

'But you love each other...'

Bethany opted to evade that statement. 'I just think that it's important not to get swept up by the fact that I'm having a baby...'

'But Cristiano's the father... What could be more natural than...?'

'I know, I know and I would never deny him his rights as a father, but we've spent so little time truly getting to know one another and it's better to stand back now than get into a situation I...*we*...end up regretting...I'm really sorry if I've disappointed you and Dad...' She shrugged her shoulders helplessly. She had spoken her piece. Without the figment of an impending marriage, Cristiano would return to London because he would have no choice and he would no longer be in a position to blackmail her into going with him *to satisfy her parents' misconceptions*. She should have been feeling the light-headed relief of a great weight being removed from her shoulders, but Bethany was assailed by a sensation of corrosive emptiness. Her success at out-manoeuvring him was a lot less satisfying than it should have been.

Furthermore, her mother couldn't understand how she

could have doubts about someone who was so spectacularly perfect. Bethany could see it on her face. Cristiano had put his best foot forward and won her over and it was horribly upsetting to think that her mother, whilst not saying anything, might actually *blame her* for being picky and unreasonable.

The atmosphere was strained by the time the front door opened and her father and Cristiano came in on a gust of sharp cold air and thick falling snow.

Bethany was ready and waiting. She had stuck on her thickest jumper, which hung down past the waist of her full gypsy skirt, her woolly hat and her fur-lined boots and hijacked Cristiano before he could make it into the kitchen, where the delicious smell of the stew was wafting out into the hallway.

'I need to talk to you,' she said, putting on her gloves and resting her small hand lightly on his arm.

'Can it wait? I need to have a shower.'

'No, it can't.' There was a vitality about him that struck her like a bolt of electricity. He might not have anticipated everything that had happened but, in fairness, he had adapted well. His world had been turned upside down and he had risen to the occasion with admirable speed. He had come up with a solution that might be inappropriate as far as *she* was concerned but it was more than a lot of men would have done under similar circumstances. And he had wormed his way into her parents' affections through a cunning combination of the gift of the gab, which always found an appreciative audience in Ireland, and a willingness to muck in.

Lord only knew how he had managed to familiarize himself with the chainsaw, but he had succeeded in chopping enough logs to last a couple of weeks and, although the snow was already piling up onto the drive, he had still managed to clear the majority of it, leaving a gritted path that was safe to walk on.

Cristiano frowned. The past few hours spent outdoors had felt good. The challenge of the land was more immediate and rewarding than he might have expected and, trudging back with John, he had allowed himself to ponder the hitherto unexplored notion that there was something deeply satisfying about the old caveman approach to life... returning to the hearth after a day of solid hard work. Big, open fire, dutiful wife, kids. Naturally, he had had to grin at his own misconception there because the last thing Bethany could be described as was dutiful.

However, he hadn't banked on returning to find her positioned by the front door like a pitbull on patrol and wearing an expression that promised a difficult end to the morning.

'The log shed's at the back of the house. I'll help you carry the logs in and we can talk.'

'Why do I get the feeling that this *talk* of yours doesn't revolve around you wanting to find out how my morning's been?' The shed which housed the logs and Ireland's trademark fuel of turf was surprisingly big and leant at an angle against the back of the house. Cristiano was only aware of the size when the final trip had been completed in silence and the last log dumped on the stack at the side. A naked overhanging lightbulb was the only form of illumination but it was enough for him to pick up the determined set of her jaw.

'Have I successfully jumped through the first set of hoops?' His mouth curled derisively. 'Or have you thought of a few more? To prove my worth?'

'You don't have to prove anything.'

'No, you're right. I don't. I'm glad you've finally reached that conclusion.' She was leaning against the side of the

shed, hands behind her back, swamped in far too many
clothes that were way too big for her. She looked small and
defenceless and vulnerable but looks, Cristiano reminded
himself, were deceiving. This was the woman who had
lied to him, had lied to her parents about him, had kept
her pregnancy a secret, something which he had unearthed
purely by chance. She had fought him tooth and nail ever
since he had arrived on the scene and even her compliance
when she had fallen into bed with him had been short-lived.
Still basking in the afterglow of their lovemaking, she had
jolted him out of his warm, pleasant drowsiness with re-
criminations and rubbish about wanting to be friends. He'd
offered her a solution to her problems, was big enough to
overlook the enormity of her deception and she threw it
back in his face. He said one thing and she immediately
made sure to say the opposite. He went in one direction,
she hived off in the other.

'I've had a long chat with my mother.' Bethany broke
the silence. It would have been more comfortable to have
had this chat in the house but she imagined that her parents
were having a little chat of their own and she wanted to
be out of the house to give them time to absorb what she
had said earlier. The log shed was the least intimate place
in the world, if you discounted its size which now, full of
fuel, placed him way too close to her for comfort but, even
so, she felt her eyes skittering over him, drinking him in.
She would have loved to have known how he'd found his
morning, was seduced by the thought of them pottering
in the kitchen, her making him tea while he regaled her
with anecdotes of battling through the frozen fields, but
she pursed her lips and, instead, said abruptly, 'I've said
that there isn't going to be any wedding.'

Cristiano had not been expecting this. He had been so

focused on a successful outcome that he hadn't appreciated that time might not have been on his side.

'And why would you do that?' He kept his voice low and soft and mildly interested, which annoyed Bethany because, under the insufferably calm exterior, she felt she could read the mindset of someone who wanted to sweep all her considerations under the carpet.

'You know why. I've already explained to you that having a baby together isn't the right reason for two people to get married.'

'And your mother wasn't curious as to the sudden decision?'

'I explained that…that we might have made a mistake, that we got involved too quickly…'

'Ah. So you stopped short of the full, undiluted truth, in other words.'

'You have to return to London, Cristiano, and it would be madness for me to go with you, but how could I stay behind if my parents believed that everything was sunshine and roses between us? I had to set them straight, so…'

He didn't say anything. Playing it cool wasn't going to work. Nor was reminding her that he had no intention of abandoning his child to an uncertain future and sporadic visits while she got on with *trying to find the right guy*.

He strolled slowly towards her and Bethany felt the fine hairs at the back of her neck begin to prickle in alarmed response.

'What…what are you doing?'

'Not fighting with you.' She might make a big deal of denying what she felt, but he could sense the desire throbbing in her, coming at him in waves. He braced himself against the back of the shed, leaning on the flats of his hands so that he was staring down at her. His anorak, unzipped at the front, hung open like two heavy curtains around her slight frame.

Bethany feverishly wondered how he could manage to make her feel so jittery and racked with nerves when he *wasn't fighting* with her. She drew in a ragged lungful of air.

'So you agree that we…we can…discuss this…um…like adults…? Now that there's no need to pretend that we're going to live out the…um…happy ever after fairy tale to my parents…?' She barely recognised her own voice.

'Sure we can…if you want.'

The clean, masculine outdoor scent of him filled her nostrils and she closed her eyes for a few seconds, breathing him in until she felt her head swimming.

His eyes were slumberous, veiled behind his thick dark eyelashes. He had a way of screening his gaze that had used to give her goosebumps because there was something outrageously erotic about it and he was looking at her like that now. Her body responded on cue. Her breasts felt heavy and the memory of how her sensitised nipples had felt the night before when he had touched them, sucked them, instantly heated her from the inside out, despite the cold weather. She wanted to back away but there was no place to back up *to*.

'Of course I…want to discuss it…you know…' She could hear herself gabbling and took a few deep breaths, which did absolutely nothing to steady her wildly beating pulse.

'Okay.'

'So…when you decide to return to London…'

'With this snow falling, it's a little hard for me to think about that just yet.' He rubbed the back of his neck and stood back. 'Tell me when exactly you want me to leave,' he said conversationally.

Faced with that direct remark, Bethany blushed and

stared down at her feet. He was done fighting for the baby. She had got what she had wanted all along. He was air-brushing himself out of the picture.

'You must be keen to be on your way,' she hedged and he looked away for a few seconds with a crooked half smile.

'You haven't answered my question.'

'Well…it'd be lunacy to try and go now. The snow… when it snows here…it's difficult to predict how long it'll last…' She was horrified to find that, having engineered his disappearance, she was now thrown into a panicky tailspin at the thought of him leaving for good. Sure, he'd return now and again, definitely to start with, and he would be brilliant with maintenance, that she knew for sure, but…

'You *do* want me to leave, don't you…?' As she hesitated on the brink of asserting her control, Cristiano placed his hands on her waist. He ignored her sharp intake of breath. He had tried being Mr Nice Guy, had chosen to give her time to come round and he was done trying now. If she wasn't going to admit to how she felt about him, then he would just have to remind her. But, this time around, he wasn't going to give her any bolt-holes. No way was she going to get the chance to erect any more barriers against him.

'Yes…you know I do…'

'Then you can creep back into your tidy little world here…' As he spoke, his hands eased under her jumper, under her shirt, found the thin stretchy fabric of her thermals. How many layers did she have on? he wondered.

Bethany emitted a noise that was halfway between a sigh and a moan. Just so long as he was standing well away from her, she could keep him at bay with reason and logic and good common sense, but the minute he touched her she went up in flames like tinder and he was touching her now. He had managed to work his way under all her protective layers and his fingers against her skin were warm and insistent, stroking her ribcage and under her breasts. She wasn't wearing a bra—her old ones were now slightly too small and she hadn't bothered to buy replacement ones.

'We're supposed…to…to be friends…' she gasped as his thumbs found the tight, firm buds of her nipples and began rubbing them in little circling movements.

'I'm finding that the friendship card doesn't work for me. I start thinking about being *friends* but I can't get the thought of you, naked and aroused, out of my head. I burn for you…' To emphasise his point, he pushed up the offending layers of clothes and cupped her swollen breasts in his hands, still rubbing her nipples and sending her into a frenzy of passion and longing.

'Stop…' Bethany pleaded shakily. 'You're not being fair…'

'I know…' Cristiano pressed her back and began kissing her neck as she arched up to meet his urgent mouth. 'That's something else that hasn't been working very well for me recently.'

Bethany whimpered softly and searched out his mouth with her eyes closed, collapsing back as he began really kissing her, his tongue moving sinuously against hers. He barely gave her time to surface and she didn't want to. She could barely keep still and her hands were tangled in his hair, pulling him down to her.

He was whispering stuff to her, snatched Italian words that were unbearably sexy, even though his voice was so low-pitched and rough that she could barely make them out.

When he paused in his hungry ministrations, a voice which she hardly recognised as her own pleaded for him to carry on.

Just this one last time, she was thinking, but even as the thought entered her head it was reduced to splinters by the bitter realisation that she would succumb over and over again. He drained her of her strength and her willpower. He, clearly, could separate lust from emotion, just as he could separate emotion from duty, but for her everything was too entwined and she hated herself for not being able to stay away from his dangerous appeal, even though she knew that it was bad for her.

'What was that?' Cristiano asked. His mouth curved into the smile of the all conquering hero.

'I don't want you to stop and I hate you for…making me say that…'

'You don't hate me. I challenge you and you feel that you need to fight against the challenge but you don't. If it's any consolation,' he continued roughly, 'you challenge me too and I've discovered that trying to fight it is no good. Why don't we stop trying to deny what we want?'

'You don't know what I want,' Bethany protested weakly.

'I know exactly what you want. Trust me.' He pulled off her woolly hat and buried his face in the abundance of her luxuriant copper hair. She always smelled of flowers, fresh and clean and somehow innocent, and he could happily lose himself just in the aroma of her.

With one hand behind her head, he set about the delicious task of plundering her mouth and with his other hand he reacquainted himself with the soft feminine curves of her body, reaching under her skirt to smooth her thighs and then to push down beneath her thick tights so that he could slip his fingers into her.

He couldn't understand what power she had over him but, from the very first time they had made love, she had made him feel like a starved man suddenly confronted with a banquet. Touching her felt *right*.

'Cristiano…no…please…' Bethany quivered as his fingers delved into the very core of her, stroking and rubbing and sending all sorts of wonderful sensations racing round her body. She had her eyes closed and her head flung back and her mouth slightly open. 'Don't stop…'

In one fluid movement, he was on his knees, her supplicant. Bethany stared slumberously at him, curled her fingers into his hair and then groaned in anticipation of what he was going to do. She felt him pull down her tights and panties and then raise her skirt. She parted her legs to accommodate him and then shuddered compulsively as his tongue replaced his deft, exploring fingers.

Her breathing sounded laboured and she wanted to cry out but couldn't. Instead, she gave little grunts of encouragement and satisfaction and twisted feverishly against his mouth as he continued to tease her with a stop/start rhythm that took her so close to the edge only to pull her back down to earth at the very last minute.

She gave a groan of utter frustration when he stood up and pressed himself against her, all the better for her to feel his hardness but, just in case she was in any doubt whatsoever, he pushed her hand against his trousers and had to clench his teeth as she felt the shape of his erection and squeezed it.

'I need *all of you*,' he growled, stilling her as she clumsily attempted to undo the zip of the trousers. 'And not here. Don't get me wrong, I've never been the sort of guy who's averse to a little kinkiness, but taking you in a shed is going a little too far…'

'We *can't go in*…!' An unseemly giggle threatened to emerge. 'Mum and Dad are in there and I…we…'

'I don't think we have much choice, my darling. We can't

strip down to our birthday suits in here and I, for one, *need* this…need *you*…' He didn't give her time to start getting her thoughts in order. Instead, he laid it on heavy by reminding her of what he wanted and needed—what they *both* wanted and needed—by closing one big hand over her breast and feathering his finger over her nipple.

He knew that he was resorting to slightly underhand tactics but he didn't really care. Nor did he stop to question the astounding fact that he was *having to resort to tactics, underhand or not.*

'We can go through the back door…I don't even know why…we're not supposed to be *doing this*…' Her hands were shaking as she straightened herself up and there was a thread of excitement uncoiling inside her. Like a teenager making use of the parents' house while they were out, she wanted to tear inside and hotfoot it to the nearest empty room. She wanted to rip his clothes off… She felt faint just thinking about it and even fainter at the thought that this was *the last thing they should be doing.* She had regaled her mother with a long speech about *reconsidering the whole marriage deal*, she had lectured him about the idiocy of sacrificing themselves for the sake of a baby, she had *positively waxed lyrical* about the fact that the best they could aim for was friendship. Since when did friends make out like a couple of sex-starved adolescents?

None of this stopped her from leaving her hand in his as they scuttled back out into the driving snow and tiptoed back into the house via the utility room door, which was always kept unlocked for easy and quick access to the log shed in the depths of winter.

In fact, the feel of his fingers curling around hers felt amazing.

They could hear the distant sound of voices emerging from the sitting room and, having removed their boots at the door, they were soundless as they hurried up the stairs, barely making it to the bedroom and shutting the door before they were on each other. Clothes, tights, underwear—everything hit the floor and was trampled underfoot as they found the bed.

'Don't go under the covers,' he growled before she could take refuge under the duvet.

'I'm fat!'

'You're beautiful.' She was. She moved him. Lying there, with her pale arms outstretched and her hair trailing across the pillow. He took his time looking at her, told her to look at him. Her stomach was decidedly rounder, her breasts fuller, her nipples bigger and darker. He could appreciate it so much better when she lay like this. It was the most erotic experience of his life. When he thought about the baby growing inside her he felt giddy. How could a man who had never given a moment's passing thought to fathering a child *feel giddy* at the thought of his baby inside her?

'So are you,' Bethany admitted unsteadily.

'A compliment…' He shot her a sexy half smile that made her toes curl. 'I like it. A lot.'

'That's because you have an ego the size of a house.' Her eyes widened, her breathing thickened as she watched him cross the shadowy room towards the bed.

'Now,' he drawled, sinking onto the bed, 'remind me where we were… Oh, yes… How could I forget…?' He parted her legs, positioned himself between them, hoisted them over his shoulders so that he was surrounded by her and, when he breathed, he breathed in the honeyed sweetness of her femininity. The way she gasped softly, as if she couldn't help the little noises emanating from her, as if she had no control over them, was a massive turn-on for him.

How could she try and push him away when they both knew that this was what they both craved?

He tasted her thoroughly and then, temporarily sated, he made his way up her body until she couldn't stand it any longer and pushed his head to her breasts, which were heavy and aching.

She had to stuff her dainty little bed cushion over her mouth to stop herself from crying out as he drew one tender nipple into his mouth and began suckling on it, tugging it tenderly, then resuming his suckling. When she reached out to touch her other nipple, he pushed her hand away so that he could switch breasts. Gazing down with hot, drowsy eyes, she could see the glistening trail his mouth left across her breasts and she closed her eyes again, luxuriating wantonly as he devoted his undivided attention to her other swollen nipple while teasing the dampness between her legs with his fingers.

'Feel good?' He looked up and his smouldering eyes locked on hers. Bethany nodded like a puppet obeying its master's controlling hand. Worse, she had no qualms of conscience about what she was doing.

She just wanted him on her, in her and with her.

He pulled her up to him when his body could no longer be restrained and then she was on top of him. Cristiano, relinquishing control, grunted as she began moving restlessly on his erection. Her breasts swayed as she moved faster and harder, driving down on him until he could bear it no longer and he groaned with a long shuddering release. He could feel her body stiffening and arching as the waves of her orgasm carried her away. Looking at her during her moment of release, the way the colour flooded her face and her eyes fluttered tightly, was enough to have him stir again in her and she sagged onto him, smiling.

'Aren't you *ever* satisfied?' she asked, stroking his chest with one finger.

'When it comes to you, it would appear not. Do you feel the same way?' His voice was lazy but his eyes were sharp as he looked down at her face against his chest.

When she nodded his satisfaction was like a shot of adrenalin.

'Good. I'm glad because this is the way it should be. Once you stop fighting me, you can start enjoying the fact that I'm going to be a permanent fixture in your life. If you don't want to marry me, then I'll respect that but know that we are still going to be together.'

'Your pregnant mistress?' There was a lump in her throat which she swallowed down.

'I prefer not to use labels when it comes to relationships,' Cristiano said, kissing her unruly hair. 'Especially when the label is *friend*. That's the one label I think you'll agree is now totally irrelevant…'

CHAPTER EIGHT

CRISTIANO had never, personally, involved himself in the tedious pastime of buying presents for women. Firstly, he didn't have time to waste dithering in shops, peering at items of jewellery and asking sales assistants for help. Secondly, he could think of nothing more soul-destroying than trying to rack his brains and come up with a suitable present for any woman. No, this was where his faithful PA had always come into her own. A woman buying for another woman. Made sense.

For the past six weeks, however, he had ditched the PA in favour of the personal touch and had found the exercise a lot less arduous than he had expected. In fact…he had discovered that there was a great deal of enjoyment to be had browsing in the shops for things that would put a smile on Bethany's face. She had quirky tastes. Having made the initial mistake of buying her jewellery, which all women presumably loved, incredibly expensive jewellery with super-watt diamonds, only to find his present politely accepted and then equally politely returned, he had revised his ideas. She didn't care for jewellery, she said, especially expensive jewellery.

'I just bet this is the sort of stuff you're accustomed to giving your girlfriends,' she had shrewdly remarked, and then had given a snort of disgust when he had defended himself on the grounds that he had never had anything returned to sender.

'Why is it,' she had asked, 'that rich men never feel the need to be imaginative?'

Cristiano, who had never failed to rise to a challenge, had become imaginative.

He had taken her to weird plays in fringe theatres, had bought her a first edition book by an Italian author which was over five hundred pages long, although he had asserted himself sufficiently to tell her that there was no way he was going to be reading it, even if he *did* speak Italian fluently, because if he couldn't get to sleep then he'd rather try his luck with a sleeping pill. But she had loved it and it had thrilled him to watch her face warm with pleasure.

He had given in to her ridiculous infatuation with a stuffed dog the size of a sofa which she had seen in Harrods and hadn't been offended when she had laughed at his scepticism and told him that he was a grumpy old man.

It seemed that there was very little she could do that offended him except for one little thing. That one tiny bump in the satisfactory progress of their relationship, namely the fact that she refused point-blank to marry him. Indeed, she had refused to move in with him, even though he had enumerated all the reasons, yet again, why it made sense, throwing into the mix the fact that they were now sleeping together; at least there was no more talk of *just being friends*. Cristiano couldn't understand it. If he was prepared to make the sacrifice, then why couldn't she? The more he had argued, the more she had dug her dainty little heels in but he had not given up. He simply resolved to get what he wanted via a more circuitous route.

Having never had to woo a woman, his attempts had not always met with resounding success. A constant conveyor belt of expensive meals out had met with a brick wall. So staying in had become the preferred option. And the kitchen, she had informed him, was a shared domain. She had bought him a recipe book and he had clumsily found himself cooking the occasional meal while he had wondered what his mother would have made of the arrangement.

Details such as those he had tactfully omitted when he had broken the news to his family. He had glossed over the lack of marriage, vaguely hinting at it as something that would happen *down the line*. He may even have let slip that Bethany was keen to walk down the aisle *after* she had given birth, when she had regained her figure. His mother had bought it but he still hoped to avoid learning what Bethany would make of that little white lie. It made no difference that the size and volume of her own lies would have put his tiny insignificant one in the shade.

Cristiano put this level of concern about her down to the fact that she was carrying his child. Under normal circumstances there was no question that things would have turned out very differently. He would have confronted her, as befitting any man who didn't like being duped. Had she not been pregnant, she would never have been able to gain the luxury of the moral high ground. The pregnancy had been the ace up her sleeve. Without it, she would doubtless have been duly repentant, would probably have thrown herself at his mercy and from that point, who knew what would have happened? It was highly likely that he would have exorcised her out of his system and returned to life as he had always known it.

As it stood, memories of his previous life seemed to belong in a very distant place.

He shopped. He was fascinated by her rapidly expanding stomach and the football games that seemed to take place inside it. He had read, cover to cover, a book on what to expect when you were expecting, which had a lot more allure, much to his bemusement, than his usual evening pastime of working. He thought about her when she wasn't with him. It seemed unnatural but he had grown to accept it.

Despite the cataclysmic change to his lifestyle, Cristiano was proud of the way he had handled the situation.

He rang the doorbell of her apartment. It was more and more ludicrous with each passing day that this was the arrangement that existed between them. Although he had settled her into the closest apartment to his that he could lay his hands on, the fact that she not only refused to marry him, for reasons which defied logic and which he couldn't begin to fathom, but insisted on separate living arrangements was a constant source of low-level dissatisfaction.

No one could tell him that she didn't enjoy sleeping with him, in positions that were frankly ingenious, taking into account her advancing pregnancy, and with penetration not always on the cards. He knew women and she wasn't faking it.

He had tactfully stopped trying to bludgeon her into an answer that made sense to him, but it still played on his mind constantly. Was this her way of keeping her options open? Was she deluded enough to think that she wasn't tied to him now? Did she really think that she could temporarily appease him, have the baby and then resume her hunt for Mr Perfect?

He was so busy scowling at the train of his thoughts that it was a few seconds before he realised that she hadn't answered the door and, at a little after seven, he couldn't think of any reason why she should be out.

He had been away for the past two days but he had spoken to her several times on the phone and she knew that he was coming over. So where the hell was she? He buzzed the bell again, this time more insistently, and at the lack of response immediately dialled her mobile. It was the most up to the minute mobile and one he had bought for her when she had moved down to London with him because he had been worried that her ancient cellphone might cut out at any given time when he might need to get in touch with her or vice versa.

He let it ring a few times, killed the connection and tried again. Worry was beginning to kick in. He raked his fingers through his hair. His instinct to break down the door was swiftly replaced by the realisation that there wasn't a hope in hell of him achieving that. The door was as solid as a slab of lead. In fact, he had had a new, exceptionally robust one put in to replace the flimsier original because, in London, you just never knew. He cursed his foresight, tried her phone again and was about to hit Plan B, which involved a locksmith, when she answered in a voice he barely recognised.

'Where are you?' was his opening demand.

'I'm here!' Bethany croaked. The doorbell had failed to wake her but the shrill ringing of her mobile had done the job. She glanced at her bedside clock and realised that she had been sleeping off and on for most of the day and into the evening.

'Where's *here*?'

'Here! In the apartment!'

'Then why the hell haven't you answered the door? And what's the matter with your voice?' He was aware of the locks being turned as he finished asking his questions and the worry which had come from nowhere and which had been dispelled the minute she had picked up her mobile slammed back into him as he took in her deathly white pallor, the shadows under her eyes and her tousled hair.

He stared down at her and panic, an emotion that was alien to him, hit him like a freight train at full speed.

'I don't feel very well.' Bethany stated the obvious as she turned and began heading back to the bedroom.

Having come straight from the airport, Cristiano grabbed his overnight bag and followed her, dumping his stuff on the ground. His heart was beating fast—too fast.

'I just need to sleep.' Bethany flopped down onto the bed and curled up under the quilt, pulling it over her head so that only her bright copper hair was visible on the pillow.

'Forget sleep. You need a doctor.' Cristiano flipped open his phone while he gently pulled down the covers so that he could feel her face. 'You're burning up. Why the hell didn't you get in touch with me?' He paused briefly to say something rapidly down the phone in Italian before snapping shut his cellphone so that he could devote one hundred per cent of his attention to her.

'You were fine when I spoke to you last night!' he told her accusingly and Bethany shot him a baleful look.

'I don't need a doctor, Cristiano.'

'Let *me* do the deciding on this one.'

'It's just a cold! A twenty-four hour bug.' She groaned and tried to submerge herself back into her warm cocoon under the duvet but he was having none of it. 'I just need to rest. And I was fine yesterday. I just got up this morning feeling a bit off-colour…'

'I spoke to you this morning and you didn't say anything.'

'You were in New York, Cristiano. What could you have done? You might think that you're capable of everything but you're not Superman. You couldn't have put on a red cape and flown across the Atlantic.'

'That's not the point.'

Bethany grunted indistinctly.

'I deserve to be kept abreast of your health at all times.' The thought of her alone in this apartment, too ill to drag herself out of bed, engendered a feeling of sick anxiety that bordered on the physical. 'You're pregnant,' he finished, standing up so that he could pace the room while cursing his friend for not already having arrived. Hadn't he told the man to get over to the apartment *immediately*?

The warm glow that had filled her at Cristiano's obvious concern dissipated like mist on a summer day. Of course he was concerned! He was concerned because she was pregnant, because she was carrying his precious cargo. The past few weeks had lulled her into a false sense of security, had seduced her into thinking that his solicitousness had been about *her*. Now those two words were a timely reminder that Cristiano only ever acted with an agenda and the agenda was about coaxing her into his way of thinking, about getting her to the point where she agreed to every proposition he ventured. She had stuck it out with insisting on having her own place, thinking that the formality of the arrangement would ensure a certain amount of essential emotional distance between them. She hadn't banked on the way he had managed to creep under all her defences.

He went shopping at the supermarket with her and he didn't complain. He bought her little things and she knew that thought had gone into the purchases. Twice he had cooked with the aid of the recipe book she had bought for him and, although the end results had borne no resemblance to the colourful, glossy pictures on the pages, he had tried. Again, without complaint. Most noticeably, he had *just been around*. She had no point of comparison on that score, but she would have put money on him being the sort of guy who always, but always, put his work ahead of everything and everyone. But he had been as regular as clockwork with her, there at the apartment by early evening, except on the occasions when he had been abroad for a couple of days and when he *had* been abroad he had called with unnerving regularity.

It had taken Herculean efforts to maintain her defences in the face of this aggressively silent onslaught but she had managed to convince herself that she had succeeded. What a fool she had been! Her crushing disappointment at the realisation that everything he had said and done had been because of their situation rather than because of *her* was ample proof that there was nothing reasonable or containable about her love.

She peeped at him from under her lashes. The sight of him literally took her breath away. It was shameful to admit, but he brought out the driven and the obsessed in her. In the middle of staring at him, he paused in his restless pacing to lock gleaming eyes on her.

'I can see that my trips abroad are going to have to be put on hold until the baby's born.' Cristiano never thought he'd see the day when his working life would take a back seat to a woman, but it appeared that that day had come. He needed to know that she was all right at all times and he knew that if he set foot out of the country then it would play at the back of his mind, like a record stuck in a groove, that some catastrophe or other might have happened about which she was keeping silent to spare him the inconvenience.

She was so obstinate and independent, despite the fact that he had managed to coerce her into moving back to London and for a few disconcerting seconds it occurred to Cristiano that those traits in her were less than ideal.

He didn't want her obstinacy, nor did he value her independence. He had always abhorred clingy, needy women but right at that moment he couldn't think of anything more rewarding than having her in a position where she would automatically turn to him for support in any crisis.

'Don't be ridiculous.'

In less than two strides, Cristiano was by the side of the bed. He didn't want to stress her out but it was suddenly imperative that he made her aware of his concerns, his *very reasonable* concerns.

'I'm not being ridiculous, Bethany. I'm being sensible. One of us has to be.'

Bethany gave an elaborate sigh that turned into a yawn. 'And naturally that role falls to you.'

Cristiano gave her a slashing smile and sat on the side of the bed so that he could half lean over her. He smoothed some of her damp hair away from her face. 'Two minutes out of the country and look what happens.'

Bethany reminded herself that this touching outpouring of concern for her welfare was just gift-wrapping around the more basic reality that he was only concerned for her because she was carrying his child but, lacking the energy for a fight, she contented herself with saying sourly, 'Like I told you, Cristiano, you're not Superman and you're not a miracle worker either. I would have got this cold whether you'd been in the country or not. I think I caught it when we were at the supermarket a couple of days ago. I stopped to chat to that little girl and she had a streaming nose. It happens.'

'You should be staying as far away as possible from anyone carrying germs!'

'What do you suggest? Maybe you could keep me locked up for the next couple of months.'

Cristiano was interrupted from informing her that it was not an unreasonable idea by the sound of the doorbell and the arrival of his friend, who he introduced as Dr Giorgio Tommasso, a man in his late thirties who, Bethany translated from the rapidly spoken Italian, was then unfairly subjected to an irate cross-examination on the lateness of his arrival.

'Just ignore him,' Bethany murmured as he sat on the bed next to her, which elicited a grin of wicked delight.

'At last,' Dr. Tommasso said, 'a woman who is capable of standing up to this brute of a friend of mine. Now, I'm going to have a listen to the baby, make sure that everything is all right…'

Like a brooding sentinel, Cristiano stood by the door and watched as his friend asked questions in a low voice, said something apparently amusing because Bethany smiled, which nearly made him remind the good doctor that he was here to examine her and not play the stand-up comic and, finally, when the examination was over, he walked towards the bed.

'Well? Diagnosis?'

'The baby's fine, Cristiano.' Dr Tommasso smiled and patted his friend gently on the arm. 'No need to get frantic.'

'I think you're confusing *being concerned* with *getting frantic*,' Cristiano said coldly. It was obvious that, even in a state of pregnancy, she was still able to charm the birds from the trees. Giorgio had a grin on his face a mile wide. What the hell was so hilarious?

'My mistake, in that case.' He struggled not to laugh as they moved towards the door. 'Bethany's got a simple case of a miserable cold. She'll feel rough for a couple of days but she's young, she's strong and she'll be fine. Her blood pressure is good and the baby's heartbeat is strong. Nothing to worry about. How are you at making soup?' His eyebrows shot up in astonishment at Cristiano's grudging reply that he saw no reason why he couldn't do that, con-

sidering his skills in the kitchen were getting better by
the day.

'I might be tempted to relay that back to your mother,
Cristiano. She won't believe that her son is finally becoming domesticated!'

Spoken in jest but a salutary wake-up call for Cristiano.
One step forward had, without him really noticing, en-
tailed two steps back as far as Bethany was concerned. No
more.

He found her in the bedroom sitting up, having just taken
some mild medication which Giorgio had told her would
make her feel better and would not affect the baby.

'Didn't I tell you?' she said, setting the glass of water
down and folding her arms. 'A simple cold. Bed rest for a
couple of days. Everything back to normal.'

Cristiano didn't reply. Instead, he went across to her
wardrobe, opened it up and cast his eye over the range of
clothes hanging up. On a shelf at the top of the wardrobe,
she had stashed her suitcase and he proceeded to remove
it in silence while Bethany watched him, open-mouthed.

'What are you doing?'

'What does it look like I'm doing?' He looked at her
briefly over his shoulder. 'Don't even think of getting up.
Bed rest.'

'You can't just start packing my case!'

'Watch me.' He strolled over to her chest of drawers and
scooped up a handful of underwear, which he proceeded
to pile on top of the clothes in the suitcase. This was followed by some random jars from her dressing table and
unidentifiable make-up, not that there was much as she
used precious little of the stuff. Task completed, he turned
around and faced her with folded arms.

'Now listen to me very carefully,' Cristiano said in a

voice as hard as granite. 'I've given this arrangement a go and it's not working.'

'It's not *my fault* that I picked up a cold!' Either the tablets she had taken had begun working with supersonic speed or else the adrenaline rushing through her body was powerful enough to disperse all her aches and pains.

Cristiano ignored her interruption. 'First and foremost, whether you like it or not, you're in no fit state to look after yourself here. You could barely make it to the front door earlier on. What if you had collapsed here on your own? Think about the consequences.'

'I would never…never do anything…' Bethany spluttered, but she paled at the picture he had cleverly painted. He had no key to her front door. She had stubbornly refused to give him one because she wanted to maintain her independence, but what if something *had* happened and he had been unable to enter the apartment? Was she so busy fighting him and fighting herself that she would risk jeopardising this baby? Was she really protecting herself or was she just punishing him because he didn't love her?

'I can't take your word on that.' He slammed shut the suitcase and yanked the zip around. 'Instead of getting in touch with me the minute you began feeling ill, you took to bed, pulled the duvet over your head and pretended that the outside world didn't exist. If you'd called, sure, I might not have been able to get here from New York in minutes, but I would have called Giorgio and he would have come over at a point when you would have been up and able to let him in. Do you see where I'm going with this? Am I spelling it out loudly and clearly enough?'

'I hate you!' Tears of bitter frustration filled her eyes. Gone was the warm man who had been worming his way through her defences. Back in his place was the cold-eyed stranger who had showed up on her parents' doorstep with a truckload of accusations.

'That's not the feeling I get when we're in bed together.'

'Is sex the only thing that matters to you?'

'It tells me that you don't hate me.' Cristiano shrugged and took out his cellphone.

He was calling his driver. Bethany listened as he directed him to collect them and from there on she would be staying at his apartment. She told herself that her stay was going to be of the minimum duration but not even that bracing thought could still the nerve-racking sensation of a net closing in around her.

'My driver will be here in an hour. Now, I think you should have a bath. It'll make you feel better.'

'I don't want a bath.'

'And you can quit sulking. It's not going to change anything.' He sauntered off in the direction of the en suite bathroom and Bethany ground her teeth together in frustration as she heard the sound of running water.

He returned a few minutes later and unceremoniously lifted her from the bed, ignoring her angry protests and carried her into the bathroom.

She liked big bathrooms. It was a legacy, she had told him in passing, from having to grow up sharing a bathroom with her sisters which had always seemed to be occupied whenever she had needed it. He had accordingly got her an apartment that had a ridiculously big bathroom, big enough to house a deep padded chair on which he proceeded to sit her down.

'Your fever's going and your colour's returned,' he said approvingly. 'But I still don't trust you to make it to the bath without falling over.'

'Don't be ridiculous!' Bethany, still smarting from his appropriation of the decision-making process and his snide reminder that she couldn't possibly hate him because they were lovers, eyed him with resentment. He ignored it.

Her head was beginning to spin. She squeezed her eyes tightly shut as he began to undo the buttons of her voluminous nightie, one of two she possessed which still fit her comfortably. She could smell the fragrance of the lavender bubble bath but she wasn't going to admit that yes, she really did want a long soak in the bath.

She also told herself that it was crazy to start being coy about her body when he was so intimately acquainted with it. Who would she be kidding? Nevertheless, as he helped her to the bath with a gentleness that was incongruous in a man as big and powerful as he was, she was acutely conscious of the weight of her breasts and the sensitivity of her nipples.

She slid into the beautifully warm water with her eyes still shut and was aware of him pulling the chair across so that he could sit alongside her.

'I'm fine now,' Bethany informed him.

'Thanks, but I'm not willing to take the chance.' Furthermore, Cristiano was enjoying her acquiescence. With no options on the table, she had been backed into a corner and he felt absolutely no guilt about that because, as far as he was concerned, he was just doing what had to be done.

Her stomach protruded above the level of the water, wet and shiny and unimaginably sexy, and so did the pouting peaks of her nipples, although he was pretty sure that she wasn't aware of that, with her eyes stubbornly closed and her mouth pursed into a tight line.

She might exude all the outward signs of frosty disapproval and maidenly outrage, but that, he knew, was only skin-deep. He would bet his vast fortune that if he bent over and took one of those tempting pink crests into his mouth she would melt faster than a candle over an open fire.

'How does that feel?' he asked, reining in his wayward thoughts when he felt his body hardening at the delectable sight of her in the bath. She did, after all, have a cold.

'I'm not going to be staying with you at your place once I'm back on my feet,' Bethany was constrained to point out and, as she opened her eyes and looked at him, he gave an elegant shrug that signified precisely nothing.

'Let me soap you. My driver will be here in a minute.'

'I'd rather not.'

'Why? Because you don't like being told what to do? Even though it's for your own good? Sit up.'

Bethany looked at him with flashing, angry eyes and he raised his eyebrows in mild amusement and reached for the soap. 'Enjoy the experience,' he drawled as she dutifully and sulkily sat up, 'because the next time I soap you it'll just be a prelude to taking you.' Did he have time for a cold shower? Probably not, but he would damn well have to have one the minute he got back to his place.

He began soaping her, taking his time as his hands slid over her shoulders and around and under her breasts.

'That's the most arrogant thing I've…I've ever heard in my life…' Her nostrils flared as his tactile fingers brushed against her nipples, which hardened in immediate response, thereby making a nonsense of her insult.

'Is it?' Cristiano murmured, reluctantly surrendering the soap back to its rightful place and standing up so that he could reach for a towel. 'Don't you like being taken care of?' His voice, as he began drying her, was like oozing, melted honey, tempting her senses and turning her brain to mush. 'I may be a dinosaur but isn't that most women's dream?'

'I don't know about most women's dream. I just know

about my own and this isn't it.' She reached for the large fluffy towel which he had put by the side of the bath and wrapped it securely and protectively around herself, still keeping her eyes firmly away from him.

Was she being greedy in wanting the dream of being loved for herself? Was that asking too much? She felt that if she released that dream then she would have nothing. Yes, he would be a responsible husband and a diligent father but, for her, it would be a sham. She didn't want a marriage based on duty or a man who would sooner or later see her as a burden.

'I refuse to rise to the bait, Bethany.' Cristiano called upon all his reserves of restraint and reminded himself that she was not feeling well, that her thoughts were probably all over the place. Yet he could feel the frustrated anger rising inside him, wanting to find a way out.

'Whatever.' She allowed herself to be helped out of the bath, which was daily becoming more of a chore for her.

'You,' he said through even, gritted teeth, 'can be the most infuriating woman on the face of the earth. I have been accommodating to the point of insanity with you, and yet you insist on throwing it back in my face.'

Bethany felt a twinge of guilt but overriding that was the thought that she didn't want an *accommodating* guy; she wanted a *doting, adoring guy who would climb the highest mountains and forge the deepest canyons for her.*

But arguing would get neither of them anywhere and she didn't want to fight with him so she kept her thoughts to herself.

'Why do you want to marry me if I'm that infuriating?' she pointed out with, Cristiano thought, an utterly feminine lack of logic. He watched in simmering silence as she dressed with her back to him and then turned and faced him with a defiant expression on her face. 'Well?' she pressed, hating herself for persisting in this and yet not wanting to let it go just yet.

'How are you feeling?'

'You haven't answered my question.'

'And I don't intend to.'

'Why not?'

'Because it doesn't deserve an answer.' He picked up her suitcase as though it weighed little more than a feather and walked towards the front door. Then he waited for her and gently held her by the arm as they headed down to his waiting driver.

'Doesn't it bother you that you're not my dream come true?' Bethany felt the sting of tears at the back of her eyes. It was a pointless exercise but she wanted to hurt him the way he was, without even knowing it, hurting her.

'Call me prosaic, but getting hyped up and emotional over romantic dreams has never been my thing.' He ushered her along to where his car was parked on a double yellow line outside her apartment block. 'We are faced with situations in life and we deal with them. End of story.' So who the hell *was* her dream guy? he wondered viciously. He was finding it hard to credit the depth of rage her wholly unjustified criticisms were arousing in him.

And he had dealt with this particular one with grace and consideration, Bethany grudgingly conceded.

'I'm beginning to feel tired.' She could feel herself wilting in the back seat of his car, drained of all her reservoirs of energy, which she had uselessly poured into arguing with him.

'My shoulder is right here,' Cristiano said gruffly. 'Lean on it.'

She did. Closing her eyes and then falling into another of her light dozes. Her brain felt muddled and tired. He wanted her to lean on him and she so badly wanted to do just that and for a few confused moments, before she drifted off, she wondered why she was bothering to fight him every inch of the way.

Was her way any more valuable than his when it came to dealing with their *situation*? He was offering her two parents for their baby and a stable arrangement. As he had reminded her on more than one occasion, they were brilliant in bed. How long that would last, she had no idea but wasn't it better to have a slice of bread rather than shout and scream because the whole loaf wasn't on offer?

The confused thoughts were still with her when the car finally came to a stop and she was lightly shaken out of her uncomfortable sleep.

She blinked sleepily and gazed up into his unswerving gaze. For a few seconds, she felt her breath catch in her throat and she straightened up and looked around her with a stifled yawn.

'You were mumbling in your sleep,' Cristiano told her. 'Care to tell me what that was all about?'

Bethany went beetroot-red but remained silent as the door was opened for her and she was helped out of the car by Cristiano's attentive driver.

All the questions which she had been asking herself when she had finally drifted to sleep were still there, nagging away at her convictions. Alongside them now, arranged like an uninvited supporting cast, was the thought of her parents, who would be over the moon if she just gave in and married the man they had welcomed and accepted like their own son…the thought of his mother who, she knew from what he had told her, would be likewise in the queue of happy people…to be joined by both her sisters, who had met and been charmed by Cristiano and flatly disparaging about her decision to wait in hope rather than marry a man who might not be the perfect guy for her…

'We need to talk,' she whispered uncertainly.

'The four least welcome words in the English vocabulary,' Cristiano remarked grimly. His hand was still around her as they rode the lift to his penthouse at the top.

'I'm thinking you won't find this talk too bad…'

CHAPTER NINE

'NO TALKING until you're in bed,' Cristiano told her, preceding her into his penthouse, which made her own sizeable apartment look like a doll's house in comparison.

The cool, imported Italian tiles, which ran through the entire floor, were liberally interrupted by the warm, vibrant colours of luxuriously expensive rugs. With virtually no doors to break the clean sweep of the sprawling apartment, the illusion of acres of space was breathtaking.

Even feeling as miserable as she was, Bethany paused, as she always did, to absorb the impact of his place.

She had never failed to marvel at the casual way with which he accepted this level of opulence. He could very well have been blind to the excruciatingly expensive originals hanging on the walls, all of which were independently worth more than most people could hope to make in a lifetime of hard graft.

He wasn't snobbish. His fabulous wealth was just an accepted fact of his privileged background and a powerful learning curve for her in understanding why he had always chosen to protect himself by knowing the pedigrees of the women he had dated. Until she had come along and blown his well thought out control measures to smithereens.

His bedroom was as impressive as the rest of the penthouse. Dark wooden shutters kept the rest of the world at bay and dominating the room was his bed, handmade because he had wanted something larger than a normal king-size. Every stitch of linen was tailored specifically to fit and the creams and chocolates imbued the space with an utterly masculine stamp.

As she obediently slid under the duvet, she noticed that the little bunch of flowers which she had impulsively bought him three days previously as a tongue-in-cheek present because his penthouse, she had told him, was just a little too relentlessly alpha male, had found their way to his bedroom and were in the process of wilting in a vase on his chest of drawers.

The sight of the flowers focused her mind and brought her tangle of thoughts together.

She had fought long and hard for her independence. She had stoutly refused to be browbeaten into marrying him because his traditionalism demanded it and she had actually thought that she had made headway because he had stopped mentioning it, but now she was tired and doubtful as to the validity of her arguments.

She had missed him when he had been away, even though she would have died rather than admit it. She had also missed his reassuring presence when she had started feeling unwell, missed the way he took control and made her feel safe. It was a joke, really, when *safe* should have been the last thing she felt around him. She had scoffed at his pig-headed insistence that marriage was the only way of dealing with their circumstances but, in truth, when she thought about him agreeing to her terms and backing out of her life, she was assaulted by a sense of driving blind panic.

The flowers gave her hope that if he didn't love her then he might just have it in him to care enough to treat her with respect when the novelty of their sexual relationship petered out for him. She held on to this fragile hope as he left, to return a couple of minutes later with a glass of water because dehydration, he informed her, was the last thing she needed. The truth was, and she couldn't make herself stifle it, maybe, just maybe, there was a chance that he could grow to feel some kind of love for her. Surely that happened! But, if it didn't happen for them, then the banquet which should have been her married life would be a plate of crumbs and she would learn to deal with it.

'So...' Cristiano sat on the bed next to her and braced himself for one of those conversations which would have him gritting his teeth in frustration and clamping down on his inclination to shout at her until she saw things his way '...you said you wanted to talk.'

'You kept my flowers.'

Cristiano followed her eyes to the chest of drawers and he flushed. 'I can't remember any woman ever buying me flowers,' he said with a shrug.

'But I bet you've bought dozens of roses for women in the past.'

'Was this what you wanted to talk to me about? Because, if it is, then it can definitely wait.'

'I...I wanted to thank you for...looking after me. If I seemed ungrateful then...'

'You're deeply sorry? Apology accepted.'

He realised how unusual it was for her to apologise. Of course, she had in the past, when he had first shown up on her doorstep and exposed her deceit, but even then her apology had bordered on challenging. Right now, she sounded sincere. He liked it. In fact, he liked it so much that he decided to work the conversation to his benefit. Ever the opportunist, he considered it a crime were he to fail to.

'It's tough always having to stand on your own,' he

murmured persuasively, taking one of her limp hands in his and distractedly playing with her fingers while he tried to mentally work out how to turn this brief moment in time, when her defences were well and truly down, to his advantage.

'Let's take tonight,' he continued softly, his dark, sexy voice rolling over her like waves lapping on sand. 'You were unwell and yes, I admit that calling a doctor might not have been strictly necessary, but isn't it reassuring to know that I care enough to do so?'

'I'm not dependent on you…'

'Of course you're not! And I would never ask you to be…' The idea, however, was an alluring one but one not to be mentioned at this juncture. 'Which isn't to say that accepting a helping hand is a sign of weakness.' The conversation seemed to be meandering and Cristiano decided to take the reins a little more firmly. No way was he going to be getting back to the value of friends rubbish she had been fond of spouting. 'We've been down this road before, Beth, but I really think it's time for you to acknowledge that it's just a hell of a lot easier dealing with this as a couple.'

He was encouraged by her lack of fighting talk. This, he thought, was more like it. He swept aside the discomforting thought that he, a man who was used to having the world at his fingertips, needed to use every trick in the book to get this woman down the aisle.

How severely he had underestimated the impact impending fatherhood would have on him!

'And think about our child.' His voice was grave. 'Should we not be man and wife, what would he think if he found out that he had been denied the privilege of both his parents because you wanted no part of it?'

Bethany frowned. 'I can't speculate that far into the future.'

'You don't have to. I can.'

She had the unnerving sensation of being under siege when, after ten minutes, he had managed to paint a picture from which she emerged as inconsiderate, thoughtless and selfish. This time round, however, she was not inclined to fight the tacit accusations, delivered by his honeyed tongue.

'Nothing to say?' Cristiano asked into the silence.

'I'm tired.'

'You should be resting,' he said immediately. He was sharp enough to know when to leave well alone. He had planted the seed and this time it appeared to have fallen on slightly more fertile ground. In due course, he would water it and he was pretty sure that it would reap its harvest eventually. Indeed, sooner rather than later. 'I'll have some food ordered in. What do you fancy?'

'Is this your way of reminding me how necessary it is to have you around, Cristiano?'

He looked suitably affronted and stood up. 'I'm only trying to do what's best and, anyway, I'm hungry if you're not. Even if you're not,' he was obliged to point out, 'you have to eat. You've probably had a lousy diet while I've been away. So what do you want? Chinese? Indian? I could get my driver to bring something from the Savoy Grill. In fact, I'll do that. You don't need greasy food. Soup and some fresh bread sound okay?'

'You don't have to.'

'Don't have to what?' Cristiano stilled, something in her voice making him feel uneasy.

'Send out for food. I'm fine with whatever you have in your fridge.'

'I've been away for two days and, before that, have

only touched base with this place. I wouldn't want to compromise your health by attempting to feed you with the contents of my fridge.'

There he went again, she thought sadly—all about the baby.

'Actually, what I meant, what I *mean*…is that you're right and you don't have to pander to my needs to get the point across. I've got it. Getting married is the sensible thing to do, so if your offer still stands, then…'

Having shamelessly manoeuvred for just this occurrence, Cristiano was reduced to a few seconds of complete and utter shock.

'In other words…' Bethany shrugged, making sure he didn't miss her concession '…you win.'

Considering he was the victor, Cristiano found that he didn't care for her phraseology, although he didn't pause to question why that might be.

'I'm glad.' In fact, ridiculously so and that was perfectly understandable, bearing in mind that he was a man who didn't like any situation that frayed at the edges. He strolled back towards her, smiling. 'In fact, I'm more than glad.'

'I'm surprised you haven't said something along the lines of knowing that I'd come to my senses in the end.'

'I knew you'd come to your senses in the end.' For someone who had been wrapped up in a million and one emotional, illogical reasons as to why she couldn't possibly commit to marriage with him, Cristiano was oddly disconcerted by her sudden change of mind. He knew that it was a conversation best left alone but he found himself sitting on the bed next to her, frowning as he tried to harness his thoughts.

'What brought about this change of heart?'

'Does it matter?'

'Possibly not, but why don't you satisfy my curiosity?'

Bethany shrugged. Now was her opportunity to show him that she could be as level-headed and downright cold as he was when addressing the delicate situation between them.

'Maybe I realised when I got ill that I'm more vulnerable than I like to think. Maybe I've just reached the point when it's time to put crazy notions aside. This is my life. I'm pregnant, for better or for worse. You've done the honourable thing by proposing marriage to me. It's the most sensible course of action, so...'

She was repeating everything he had said to her in the past, virtually word for word, but Cristiano felt unsettled and disproportionately angry at her resigned acquiescence.

'All true.' His voice was clipped and matter-of-fact. 'I just wonder what happened to all the romantic notions of not wanting to be tied down with the wrong guy.' *The wrong guy.* Never had three words left a more bitter taste in his mouth.

He also couldn't work out why he wasn't more upbeat about this. He had spent long enough canvassing for such a result, after all. Yet, in possession of the spoils, he now perversely thought that the least she could do was show a bit more enthusiasm. He'd spent weeks bending over backwards to accommodate her and yet none of that appeared to have been taken into account.

Bethany worried her lower lip. Cristiano, whose strong, aggressive personality had been predictable in one area only, and that was in his desire to have her firmly wedded to his side to fulfil his prehistoric notions of conventionality, was now responding in a way that brought her out in a fine film of nervous perspiration. He had told her that he was glad, that he was *more than glad*. But he wasn't looking very glad.

The thought that he might have changed his mind, that he might, actually, have come round to *her* way of thinking, despite everything he had said in the past, made her feel sick. Had he just been going through the motions of presenting the marriage option as the one and only solution to what he saw as a shared problem, in the vague expectation that she would continue rejecting his offer, giving him the chance to claim the pious moral high ground in the years to come? He had insisted on her moving in with him. Maybe he saw that as a necessary step at a time in her pregnancy when she needed to have him around. Maybe, without even realising it, he had already accepted that the move would be temporary, until the baby was born, at which point he would, of course, remain a dutiful and generous presence in the life of his child and probably to her as well, but perhaps her insistence on maintaining their respective freedom had begun its gentle process of eroding his convictions that a child required both parents on site.

She wanted to backtrack, to tell him that if he'd changed his mind then that was *perfectly all right*.

Instead, she said coolly, 'I wasn't thinking in a practical way. If you're still interested in marriage, then I'm willing to submit but with a few provisions of my own.'

Willing to submit? Provisions? Anyone would think that he had threatened torture instead of a lifetime of having anything she could possibly want!

'And what, exactly, might these provisions be?' Cristiano asked blandly.

'I realise that it'll be a marriage of convenience, but… but…' She fiddled with the duvet and then stared down fixedly at her fingers while she tried to catch her breath and sound as normal as possible. Two adults being sensible. 'I don't expect you to…start playing the field the second you get tired of playing Happy Families…'

Cristiano's eyes iced over. He walked over to the window, buying himself a bit more time so that he could control the volcanic fury rising in him. 'What sort of person do you think I am?' he asked in a voice as smooth and as sharp as a razor blade. 'How sleazy do you think I am?'

'I don't think you're sleazy.' Bethany stuck her chin up and glared at him. 'I think you're a man who has... needs...and, when you get bored with me, then you might be tempted to stray...'

'Then you'll have to make sure that life never gets boring, won't you?' It was a pretty sleazy remark, considering he had professed outrage at the description, but Cristiano wasn't ashamed of himself. This wasn't what he had expected when he had envisaged his plans for them both finally coming to fruition.

'Is that a threat?' Bethany asked tautly. 'Do whatever you want or else you find someone else?'

'You're putting words into my mouth and I don't appreciate it.'

'Well, *excuse me* for just trying to lay down some boundaries here, in so far as they'll affect my life!'

'You're not laying down boundaries. You're bracing yourself for failure.'

'That's not the way I see it and if you won't agree to this small thing then it's probably better that we do the best we can with a custody arrangement.'

Cristiano wondered how it was that she had such a knack of saying precisely what he didn't want to hear. Just the words *custody arrangement* ratcheted up his outrage, bringing to mind as it did visions of her with another man. He made a Herculean effort to control his temper. She had agreed to marry him, albeit gracelessly, and he would work with that.

'We marry,' Cristiano stated flatly. 'I won't fool around

and neither will you. Moreover, you will throw everything you have into making our marriage work. I will not tolerate anything that reeks of being a sham.'

Bethany took that to read that, as far as the outside world was concerned, they would present the image of the perfect couple. She knew that it was now or never. Agree and her fate was sealed. Object and he would no longer bother trying to convince her to walk down that road with him. He would see her through the pregnancy and then he would step back. Not from his child, but from her.

It angered her to finally admit to herself that she didn't want him to be with any other woman. She couldn't bear the thought of him looking at anyone else, speculating about what it might be like to have sex with them.

Bethany nodded and didn't say anything. When she next sneaked a look at him, he appeared more relaxed. He pulled out his mobile phone, dialled into it and handed it over to her.

'Your parents. Time to break the good news to them. I will then let my mother know.'

'Already?' Her voice was high-pitched and nervous but she could feel a treacherous thread of excitement fluttering through her. Her hands were shaking as she took the phone from him.

Fifteen minutes later, she returned the phone to him. He had remained in the bedroom, standing with his legs slightly apart, his arms folded and giving the impression that he was making sure that she didn't chicken out at the last minute.

'Your turn.'

Cristiano scowled. She had complied with his wishes but there was a tension between them that had been absent since she had moved back to London. He felt as though she had given in, accepted the unacceptable and the mere fact of it now stuck in her throat. Thanks to him, she had been forced to relinquish her romantic dreams and bow to practicality. The notion that they might actually *be happy* did not seem to figure anywhere on her horizon, never mind that they had been perfectly happy before, in bed and out of it, for that matter.

'I will call later. And there's no need to look so miserable about the prospect of marrying me. I'm going to be giving you all the security you could possibly hope for.' He looked at her with brooding frustration.

'I know.' *Security!* When marriage should have been a joyful exchange of love, he offered her security. She hated herself for loving him so much that she was willing to compromise the principles she held dear. She hated herself for knowing that, however inadequate any marriage to Cristiano might be, it would still be better than living apart from him, seeing him on appointed days, watching from the sidelines while he inevitably hooked up with another woman, maybe one who he went on to fall in love with. And she hated the unpalatable truth that if she didn't marry him he would get bored with her sooner or later, at which point she would have no hold whatsoever over him and, without him in her life, she would be rudderless.

She would always be faithful to him because she had no choice. She was a prisoner of her own ungovernable emotions. He, on the other hand, whilst professing to be insulted that she would even think of confining him to a life of fidelity, would have no such emotional ties. She would be condemned to a life of never really trusting that he wouldn't stray. How many men, with a libido as powerful as his and the sort of sexy, magnetic pull that had women swinging round for a second look, would embrace monogamy once the novelty of a wife who had been forced on him began to fade? He wanted her *now*, he found her pregnancy sexy *now* but, when it came to calendars, *now* was over in the blink of an eye.

And there he was, frowning at her and ordering her to look happy!

Worse than that, she wanted to smooth the frown from his face and she had to fight against the temptation to beat herself up for putting it there.

'You were happy.' Cristiano issued that as a statement of fact.

Bethany flushed because yes, she *had been*. Happy in the little bubble they had created since their return from Ireland. She had had the one hundred per cent attention of a very devoted Cristiano. Now she felt oddly confused instead of at peace with her decision.

'What's changed?' he asked. He was finding it difficult to comprehend her new mood. They had good sex, she had accepted his proposal of marriage. So why the hell did she look as though she had found a penny and lost a pound? He raked his fingers through his hair and began pacing the room.

'Nothing,' Bethany whispered miserably. She lay back and closed her eyes, shutting him out because it tore her heart in two just to look at him.

After a while, she forced herself to open her eyes and give him a wobbly smile. 'What about that soup and bread you were talking about?'

Cristiano was oddly reluctant to let go of their conversation although he didn't know where he expected to get by pursuing it. He had forced her to marry him, of that he was in little doubt, had laid down one or two ground rules of his own, which was important. If he had come across as tyrannical, then it was for her own good, as she would discover in the fullness of time. Of that he was certain. Any thought that he might have behaved differently was

not allowed to surface because the more time he had spent
with her, the more convinced he had become that he wanted
her exclusively to himself. He permitted himself to return
her smile because there was no sense in dragging out an
uncomfortable situation. He had already got a grudging
admission that she had been happy with him. He saw no
reason why she wouldn't be happy again.

'I will set things in motion,' he said softly, content to
have reasoned himself out of his peculiar mood. 'A small
wedding, I think… Wouldn't you agree? Although, of
course, if you feel strongly about having the whole big tra-
ditional thing, then I will be more than happy to oblige.'

'Dress in white and about to give birth… It doesn't work,
does it?'

'It would work for me,' Cristiano said roughly. 'But then
so would pretty much anything else.'

Bethany's face suffused with colour. The black cloud
that had been hanging over him had been shrugged off.
He was back to his normal self. Did that mean that he was
really happy that they were getting married? He was so
much better at concealing his emotions than she was.

'Now,' he said, before his eyes began drifting and his
body began following suit, which it always seemed to do
whenever he was around her. 'Food and then sleep.'

Bethany sipped her coffee and stared out idly at a scene
of London in the throes of Friday lunchtime shoppers and
workers making the most of their hour away from the desk.
She, herself, with only a couple of weeks left of her pregnancy to go, was far too big to do anything as dramatic
as shopping. She was still determined to walk as much as
was comfortable, which got her as far as the patisserie in
the square just off the King's Road, and she had developed
the pleasant habit of having a cup of coffee and her lunch

there. From her vantage point behind glass, she could muse on her impending wedding, due to take place three months after the baby was born, while the rest of the world went about its business.

Cristiano, who preferred to have things done slightly faster than the speed of light, had peremptorily assumed that they would be married just as soon as he could arrange someone to physically marry them, but Bethany had stood firm. She only intended to be married once and she wasn't going to submit to a rush job even though the marriage might be one of convenience. She wanted to pretend to herself that it was the real deal. Since when was that a crime?

A couple in front of one of the high end shops were arguing with one another and Bethany followed their angry hand gestures while she lost herself in her thoughts.

She had pretty much given up trying to hang on to any defence system with Cristiano. With the single-minded focus that was so much a part of his driven, assertive personality, he had set about proving himself indispensable. He was attentive, he was supportive, he was everything she could have hoped for and if he never, ever, not once told her that he loved her, then it was a telling omission to which she never alluded. In return, she kept her feelings to herself and quietly gave in to the crazy hope that he would, suddenly and miraculously, decide that he was in love with her.

To the outside world, he certainly gave every impression of it. The weekend spent in Ireland with her parents only recently had seen him the very embodiment of the devoted husband-to-be and she was pretty certain that when she met his relatives in two weeks' time he would project the same image.

Bethany, however, did not want to go down this particular road. The minute she started thinking about the stark reality of their situation she could feel herself begin to flounder and panic and she had become adept at shoving all her uncomfortable thoughts to the back of her mind.

The arguing couple had moved off. Bethany glanced down at her watch, thinking of the wall to wall meetings that Cristiano would be facing today while she loitered with her savoury pastry and her hot chocolate. He would be back late, he had told her, because his schedule was packed tighter than sardines in a tin.

She looked up, half smiling because just thinking of him made her feel like a giddy teenager and, as her eyes focused, she blinked and leaned forward, dropping the pastry back onto the plate.

Her heart began to thud as she recognised Cristiano, so impossibly distinctive in his impeccably tailored Italian suit, one hand thrust into his trouser pocket where he would be idly jangling whatever loose change happened to be there because that was one of his little habits. He was laughing, leaning into the petite blonde woman standing in front of him and he was concentrating on whatever she was saying with every fibre of his being. Because that, too, was just something that he did.

Bethany felt her breathing become laboured. Her eyes slid away from him to look at the woman he was with. She had a gamine face, big eyes and her blonde hair was cut close to her head. It was a style she could pull off. She looked like a very pretty tomboy with her saddle style bag slung over one shoulder and her sneakers and combats.

Cristiano was supposed to be at meetings all day. He didn't have a window, he had told her. Some big deals were on the brink of coming to fruition, he had told her. He had kissed her on her nose and drawled, with lazy amusement because he knew that his remark would be provocative, that she shouldn't worry her pretty little head about any of it, then he had transferred the kiss to her mouth and told her how tempted he was to ditch the deals and climb back into bed with her.

Clearly whatever deals he had had were wrapped up in attractive little packages, which was a little technicality he had omitted to mention.

She was so focused on the tableau taking place where the couple had earlier argued that she only realised how tightly her fists were clenched when the soft palms of her hands began to hurt from the pressure of her fingernails. She came close to passing out as he took the blonde's arm with what looked to her as way too much familiarity and then strode off, still smiling, still looking *bloody pleased with himself.*

The monster that she had become accustomed to thrusting to the back of the cupboard jumped out and grabbed her by her throat. This was what she had feared. Having got her in the position he had wanted from the very beginning, he was already beginning to appreciate that the world was full of women. Did the girl work with him? For him? It didn't matter. All that mattered was that he had lied to her and the lie was loaded with significance. What sort of meeting took place close to the chic cafés off the King's Road? What sort of businesswoman dressed in combats? The secretive sort, it would seem, that he couldn't tell her about.

She spent the next few hours in a state of emotional meltdown and when, at a little after ten, she heard the sound of the front door opening and slamming shut, her entire body tensed.

He was tugging off his tie as he strolled into the bedroom. He walked straight across to her, for all the world as if absolutely nothing was wrong, as if it had all been just another day at the office and shot her one of those trademark sexy smiles that made every bone in her body go to liquid.

'You're up.' He stated the obvious. He leant over the bed, where her book was resting comically on her protruding stomach, and deposited a kiss on her mouth.

The smell of him was so intensely satisfying, so uniquely *him*, that she almost returned the kiss.

'Good day?'

'Busy. I'm going to have a shower. Don't move a muscle. I'll be out in fifteen minutes.'

He didn't close the door to the adjoining bathroom, nor was he modest when it came to disrobing in front of her and her eyes lingered on him with sickening hunger until she looked down and lay on her side, the only comfortable position for her now.

Cristiano, shower finished, exited the bathroom with his towel slung low round his waist and paused by the door. He was acutely attuned to her every mood and right now his antennae were telling him that something was wrong. He didn't like it. His days of fundamental indifference to how women interpreted his behaviour was a thing of the past.

He walked slowly towards the bed and circled so that he was in her reluctant line of vision.

Bethany stared at the unnerving sight of his legs in front of her and the bottom of the white towel which only paid lip service to the task of concealing his impressive manhood.

She had had a few hours to work out how she was going to deal with what she had seen. She had contemplated saying nothing and had rejected that option because the *not knowing for sure* would eat away at her like a cancer. But she wasn't going to get hysterical. Cristiano didn't do drama. She rolled over onto her back and heaved herself up into a semi-sitting position.

'Have you eaten?' she asked, her eyes fluttering away from the magnificent sight of him which, she realised with dismay, could still make her feel weak and gooey inside, even though that was a sensation she desperately wanted to suppress.

'There were sandwiches tonight round the conference table.' Cristiano stared down at her taut frame, the way her eyes were skittering away from him. 'You're tiptoeing round something. Why don't you just come right out and tell me instead of working yourself up into a lather?'

'How did you spend your day?'

Cristiano shook his head impatiently and walked towards his chest of drawers, dropping the towel en route and shrugging on a pair of boxers. 'I worked. That's what I do. I sat opposite boring men in suits poring over reports, checking legal documents and signing off on deals. In between I kept my eye on the shares index so that I could head off any potential investment crises. At eight-thirty one of the secretaries went out to buy some sandwiches. I ate two. I came home. You were upbeat when I left you this morning. I did not envisage returning to find you in a mood.'

'I'm not in a mood. I'm just trying to find out how you spent your day.'

'And now you have. Unless you'd like me to elaborate on some of the more tedious details.'

'Maybe just one,' Bethany told him, taking in a deep, steadying lungful of air.

Cristiano sighed and looked at her wryly. He had no idea where she was going with this but he would humour her. She was big with his child and she was his wife-to-be. All normal rules of play were suspended.

'Can't wait to hear.'

'What were you doing at lunchtime with another woman? And don't try to deny it. I saw you.'

CHAPTER TEN

CRISTIANO stilled. He was hanging on to his temper with restraint because he didn't want to stress her out, but no one had ever questioned his movements before.

'I don't have to deny anything,' he said. Habit born from a lifetime of being unanswerable to anyone slammed into place. He wasn't going to be cross-examined by *anyone*. It smacked of being under the thumb and yes, he had altered a lot for this woman but enough was enough. Lines had to drawn, essential boundaries established.

His words shattered every fragile hope that there would be a perfectly reasonable explanation for what she had seen and Bethany felt as though she had been delivered a physical blow.

'You're too much, Cristiano,' Bethany whispered. 'You're just too much.'

'What is *that* supposed to mean?'

'It means that I can't go through with this marriage with you.'

'This is ridiculous.' He was keeping his voice low and reasonable but it was a feat of willpower. 'And you don't need to get worked up at this point in time.'

'I'll get worked up if I want to get worked up!' Everything came down to her health because she was carrying his baby! Tears of bitterness and disappointment and frustration trembled on her lashes and she pursed her lips to avoid the disadvantage of becoming emotional.

Cristiano gritted his teeth together. 'Is this it, Bethany? Am I to be subjected to a change of mind every single time you get a little down over something?'

'I'm not *getting a little down*, Cristiano! I'm just asking you to explain why you lied to me about where you were today. Is that asking too much?'

'It's telling me that you don't trust me,' Cristiano said quietly. 'You're accusing me of having an affair and I'm telling you that I'm not. I don't see why there should be anything further said on the matter.'

So why, Bethany wondered, wouldn't he tell her exactly what he had been up to with the woman she had seen him with? If he was as innocent and as pure as the driven snow, why the secrecy? Maybe he was *technically* telling the truth. Maybe he wasn't involved in some kind of rampant sexual situation with the woman but what if he was *playing with the idea*? Maybe he didn't count *flirting* as infidelity, but *she* did. She didn't want him to even *look* at another woman. Ever.

Her thoughts clamoured in her head like a thousand squabbling voices. She tried to get hold of a little reason and common sense. She knew that he was right in so far as she couldn't chop and change her mind about marrying him like a leaf blown about in a high wind. But he didn't love her so how could she, ultimately, trust him?

'Fine,' Bethany muttered miserably.

She had retracted her claws, Cristiano acknowledged, but not for long. He knew this woman like none other, knew her well enough to recognise her determination when it came to getting answers. Indeed, she was very much like him in that respect. But he wasn't going to be browbeaten in this instance. He bracingly told himself that however much he was responsible for her well-being and however honourable a man he was when it came to doing his duty, he was not about to be emasculated by anyone demanding detailed reports on him to satisfy her feverish imagination.

He had done nothing wrong, end of story.

Arriving at this irrefutable truth should have instantly restored his mood, but Cristiano found that he was still weirdly out of sorts.

'It's late,' he said abruptly. 'And arguing into the early hours of the morning isn't going to do you any good. You need your sleep.'

'Stop telling me what I need and what I don't need.'

'Why? I'm right.' He said that as though it was a truth written in stone.

'For *right*, read *arrogant*.' How could he stand there and treat her like a child throwing a temper tantrum over nothing? Would that be the way he intended to treat her in the future? To every concern she might voice, would he just always say, *Trust me, I'm right*?

She had made her bed and she knew that she would lie in it, but she couldn't stop herself from thinking about the woman who had been smiling up at him. If she had been dressed in a suit, if she had looked the part of the businesswoman, then Bethany might not have had such a hard time believing him, but what businesswoman dressed in combat trousers?

Like a record stuck in a groove, she kept replaying the scene in her head until she wanted to burst into tears.

Cristiano was watching her carefully. Her body was as rigid as a piece of board. He couldn't understand why she was making such a fuss over nothing but, driven into a corner, he refused to unbend. Instead, he said in a conciliatory voice, 'I'm going to go to the study and work for a while. Leave you to calm down.'

'I don't *want* to calm down! I want to talk.'

'You either trust me or you don't. Yes, I met a woman at lunchtime. No, I am not sleeping with her. Now, I'm going to leave you on your own to get some sleep. Don't be concerned if you wake and I'm not here. I think I might sleep in one of the spare rooms tonight.'

As soon as he had left the room, Bethany succumbed to a flood of hot tears.

Had she been wrong? She had wanted answers and no one could say that that had been unreasonable, but if she had been right, then how was it that she now felt as though the bottom of her world had dropped out?

She resisted the temptation to follow him to his study and pick up where they had left off, but pride glued her to the bed and, besides, would he say anything different from what he had already said? Cristiano was fiercely independent and ran his life according to his own personal laws, which were always fair. He had conceded much on her behalf. She remembered his revised timetable which had seen him with her at times that would have surely gone against every workaholic gene in his body. He had accused her of mistrust and her brain had shrieked that mistrust was always going to be an issue when he didn't love her, but she couldn't imagine Cristiano sneaking around behind her back. Which, in turn, brought her back to the same old questions and the same old fears.

Added to this horrible mix was an element of doubt. When had Cristiano ever lied to her? In fact, when it came to that particular trait, it was fair to say that *she* was the main culprit. Yet she had not hesitated to accuse him of lying or at least of concealment.

She finally fell asleep, disquieted by the fact that somehow, somewhere, the conversation had turned and she had been left feeling the guilty party.

She surfaced the following morning at the ungodly hour of seven-thirty to find that his side of the bed had not been slept in.

Panic gripped her and she stumbled through her ablutions, which now took much, much longer because of her unwieldy girth.

Where was Cristiano? Despite her troubled thoughts, she had slept like a baby, despite her awkwardness lying down. She had not heard him enter the room at any point. Had he been true to his word and slept in the guest room? There was no sign of him in any of the guest rooms. Perhaps he had gone to work early.

She was dialling his number with trembling fingers as she walked out of the bedroom and she almost fainted in relief when he picked up on practically the first ring.

'Where are you?'

Cristiano heard the urgency in her voice with a deep sense of satisfaction. Direct inquisition had disagreed with him, but he had felt no better having stood firm on his resolve not to have his movements questioned. In fact, he had spent the night feeling as though he had been punched in the gut. At some ridiculous hour in the morning he had sneaked into the bedroom and looked at her. It felt all wrong not to slide into the bed next to her, but he hadn't wanted to risk waking her up. Hadn't wanted to take the chance that she might surface to resume her argument with him.

'You're up.'

'Where are you? You haven't answered me.'

'Give me a minute.'

Bethany heard the dull burr of a phone that had gone dead and she snapped shut the lid of her cellphone. Her heart was beating like a hammer. She glanced down at the cellphone in her hand and, when she looked up, it was to see him standing in the kitchen. She hadn't heard him but he must have been working in the study at the end of the apartment. Relief at just *seeing him* nearly blew her off her feet. She wanted to race over to him, fling herself into his arms, tell him how much she loved him.

'Sleep well?' she asked instead, looking at him cautiously as he strolled towards her. He was absolutely gorgeous. She wondered whether, one day, she might become accustomed to the immense physical impact he always contrived to have on her. He wasn't smiling, which made her nervously wonder if he was still brooding on their argument of the night before. Right or wrong, she realised that she didn't want that.

How far would she go, she wondered, in accepting whatever Cristiano chucked at her? Because she loved him? Experience was fast telling her *very far indeed*.

'No.'

That single word jolted her out of her painful musings. 'You don't look like a man who's had a restless night.'

'I scrub up well.'

'What…were you doing?' She hated herself for asking the question but she unhappily heard herself ask it anyway.

'I worked for the better part of the night. Right here, to forestall your next question. On my own.' Cristiano had had hours to think about their argument. He had had hours to analyse his initial response to her questioning and minutes to conclude that really, far from being driven into a corner, which was a place he didn't care for, he had *liked* it. He had *liked* the fact that she had been jealous because from jealousy came need and need was a very good thing in her. Habit had conditioned his initial response. It was time to say goodbye to habits, even the old ones that took the longest to die.

'Come and sit down,' he said, urging her into the kitchen. 'I'll make you some breakfast.'

'Why?'

'Aren't you hungry?'

'I mean why aren't you mad at me?' She wondered if he thought that she might suddenly go into premature labour if she became too stressed out. His concern usually centred on making sure that she was in tip-top shape with the pregnancy.

'Why should I be?'

'Because…because…' She found herself seated at one of the bar stools in the kitchen, watching as he deftly whipped up some scrambled egg on toast for her. She wasn't entirely sure how she had got there.

'You had every right to ask me what I was doing in the company of another woman.' Cristiano placed the plate of toast and egg in front of her and pulled one of the chairs around so that he could sit on it facing her as she dabbled with her fork, ostensibly not meeting his eyes, until he gently tilted her face up.

'You either have to eat or else look at me. You don't have the option of doing neither.'

Bethany chose to concentrate on her food. He had become a dab hand at cooking certain basic dishes. Scrambled eggs was one of them.

'I *do* trust you,' Bethany mumbled between mouthfuls, her face burning. 'It's just that I was…' While she racked her brain to think of an adjective that wouldn't reveal the level of her obsession with him, he jumped in to supply it.

'Jealous?'

There was a whisper of silence and she put down her

fork, staring down at her plate, which seemed the only safe point on which to focus. His hand covered hers and she risked a glance at his face.

'I'd be jealous of you too,' he admitted roughly.

'You…would?'

'Hell, yes.'

'That's because you're the kind of guy who sees women as possessions.' She made her excuses for his confession lest she begin playing with the seductive fantasy that it meant more than he intended.

'You couldn't be further from the truth, in actual fact.' He stood up abruptly and removed the plate, which seemed to have acquired mesmerising qualities for her. He didn't want her mesmerised by anything or anyone but him.

'I won't pretend that I haven't had my fair share of women,' he began, his back to her as he roughly washed the plate followed by the saucepan and pieces of cutlery. Then he turned round so that he was looking directly at her, leaning against the counter, his feet loosely crossed at the ankles. He shrugged as her eyes flickered towards him and he noted that glint of jealousy again. However hard she tried to hide it, it seeped out of her and she was obviously innocently unaware of how intoxicating he found it.

'And I've never allowed any woman to dictate terms and conditions to me.'

'I wasn't dict…'

'Shh. Let me finish.' He nodded towards the sitting room and waited until she was settled comfortably on the sofa before sitting next to her to continue. 'I've always led a life conducted on *my* terms. Women had the choice. Abide by my rules or quit. My rules were simple. Work came first and there were to be no scenes. No hissy fits, no possessiveness, no wanting more than I was prepared to give.'

Totting up the number of rules she had broken on his

magical list made Bethany feel a bit faint. She had also *got* onto his list, in the first instance, by breaking the cardinal rule number one, which had to be *no deception*. He had shown remarkable resilience in the circumstances but had he now run out of patience with her?

Cristiano leaned forward, his elbows resting on his knees. He raked his fingers through his hair and shot her a baffled sideways glance that had her nerves frantically racing.

'Okay. So maybe I broke one or two of your...'

'Forgot another rule. No interrupting. Not when I'm trying to figure out how to say what I have to say.'

'Which is...?' Bethany's voice was a shade above a whisper.

'Which is...' Cristiano looked at her. There was a strange, swooping sensation inside him. It alternately made him feel terrified, exhilarated and absolutely convinced that this was where he was finally destined to be. 'Which is...that you are allowed to break every rule in my book. In fact, if I'm not mistaken, you've already ridden roughshod over most of them and I've discovered that I don't care.'

'You don't have to say stuff like that.'

'What do you mean?'

'I mean, I know that you don't want to upset me because I'm pregnant, but that doesn't mean that you have to...have to...'

Cristiano gave a smile of such immense warmth and tenderness that Bethany drew in her breath unsteadily.

'You're beautiful. Have I told you that? You pulled me in hook, line and sinker from the very first minute I laid eyes on you. Even when I stormed over to Ireland to confront you, you were irresistible.'

Bethany didn't say anything. Actually, she didn't want to breathe for fear of disturbing this frank outpouring of emotion. She never wanted this moment to end. She wondered if it would destroy the mood if she told him that he was beautiful too.

'I should have been gutted when you told me that you were pregnant. I had never anticipated my lifestyle changing. On the few occasions I thought about marriage and children, I foolishly imagined that my life would carry on without major interruptions. A suitably docile wife would hover somewhere in the background, doing whatever needed doing on the home front, leaving me free to remain exactly the way I'd always been.'

Bethany was fascinated by the vulnerability she saw on Cristiano's face. She reached out to touch him and he clasped her hand tightly in his.

'When you offered me the uninterrupted choice, however, I found that there was no way I was going to take it. I wanted all of you.' He looked at her steadily. 'I didn't want to be a part-time father and I definitely didn't want to be a part time fixture in your life. Okay, this is really hard for me to say and I've never said it before, but I love you. I think I fell in love with you over those two weeks in Barbados but hell, how was I supposed to know that? I'd never felt that way before and, to tell you the truth, I didn't figure that love could be wrapped up in such a bloody unpredictable, turbulent package. I called it lust and thought it was a passing affliction. Then I called it duty. I gave it every name under the sun but the right one.'

'You *love me*?'

'Don't sound so shocked,' Cristiano told her defensively. 'Everything I've done over the past few months has proved it.'

And it had. Bethany threw her arms around him and would have told him a thousand times over that she loved him too if he hadn't stopped her, laughing.

'I am sorry I didn't explain about Anita,' he said eventually.

'You felt cornered,' Bethany mused slowly. 'I wasn't trying to be a horrible, nagging shrew.'

'You have every right to be a nagging shrew. I'd rather that than thinking that you wouldn't care if you saw me with another woman because if I ever saw you with another guy I'd grind him to a pulp.'

Still on cloud nine, Bethany learned that Anita, the wearer of the combat trousers who had given rise to such drama and soul-searching, was a coordinator for charity work in Africa.

'I wanted to surprise you when I told you. I'm now involved in building a community village centre in Central Africa. It's to be the first of many.' He grinned at her open-mouthed expression of surprise. 'Don't look so stunned,' he told her, holding her close and depositing a loving kiss on her mouth. 'Didn't you tell your parents, after all, that I'm involved in charity work all over the world…? You can help me decide where my next project will be…considering you're the instigator… And, by the way, you have nothing to fear from Anita. She's gay.'

Cristiano and Bethany's baby daughter was born without any drama two weeks later. Cristiano announced, with an earnest sincerity that made Bethany laugh, that he had fallen in love all over again. Helena Grace was plump, with her mother's copper hair and her father's lustrous dark eyes and those amazing eyelashes. Grandparents descended and fussed over the first grandchild for both lines, wedding plans were discussed in detail, with Cristiano and Bethany watching on with amusement and contributing as required and neither could wait until they found their bed at night. With their baby often between them, before she was gently transferred to her Moses basket at the side of the bed, her tiny fists curled tightly as she slept, they softly discussed leaving London for somewhere with commuting distance but less hectic.

'I never thought,' Cristiano mused more than once, 'that I would live to see the day when I would want to escape the frantic pace of working life in London. This is your fault, my darling witch…'

Bethany was all too happy to take the blame.

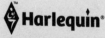

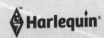

Harlequin Super Romance®

...there's more to the story!

Superromance.
A *big* satisfying read about unforgettable characters. Each month we offer *six* very different stories that range from family drama to adventure and mystery, from highly emotional stories to romantic comedies—and much more! Stories about people you'll believe in and care about. Stories too compelling to put down....

Our authors are among today's *best* romance writers. You'll find familiar names and talented newcomers. Many of them are award winners— and you'll see why!

If you want the biggest and best in romance fiction, you'll get it from Superromance!

Exciting, Emotional, Unexpected...

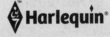

Harlequin®

A *Romance* FOR EVERY MOOD™

www.ReaderService.com

HSRDIR11

INTRIGUE®

BREATHTAKING ROMANTIC SUSPENSE

Shared dangers and passions lead to electrifying romance and heart-stopping suspense!

Every month, you'll meet six new heroes who are guaranteed to make your spine tingle and your pulse pound. With them you'll enter into the exciting world of Harlequin Intrigue— where your life is on the line and so is your heart!

THAT'S INTRIGUE— ROMANTIC SUSPENSE AT ITS BEST!

A *Romance* FOR EVERY MOOD™

INTDIR11

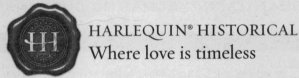

HARLEQUIN® HISTORICAL
Where love is timeless

*Imagine a time of chivalrous knights
and unconventional ladies,
roguish rakes and impetuous heiresses,
rugged cowboys and
spirited frontierswomen—
these rich and vivid tales
will capture your imagination!*

HARLEQUIN HISTORICAL...
THEY'RE TOO GOOD TO MISS!